Sundaes and
Cove Cozy Mystery Series Book 9

By Leena Clover

Chapter 1

The seaside town of Pelican Cove was ablaze with spring flowers. Pink and white blossoms adorned cherry trees and dogwoods, perfuming the air with a heady fragrance. The sun shone brightly, a clear harbinger of warmer weather, making the grumpiest person smile.

A lively conversation was in progress at the Boardwalk Café. A group of women sat out on the deck, braving the slight chill that lingered inspite of the brilliant sunlight. They were a diverse bunch, with 80 something year old Betty Sue Morse their undisputed leader. Her knitting needles clacked in a rhythm as she twirled strands of lavender and white wool over them.

"You think Emily will love these booties?" she asked, gazing adoringly at the bonny baby sitting in a high chair.

Emily clapped her hands when she heard her name and babbled something as she chewed on a fist.

"Of course she's going to love them," Jenny King said, smiling at the baby. "Aren't you, sweetie?"

She kissed the baby's cheek and offered her a tiny bit of the muffin she was eating.

"Is Emily going with us?" Heather Morse, a young

woman in her thirties wanted to know. "She might cramp your style, Jenny."

"Mind what you say about my baby girl," Jenny warned her.

Jenny's aunt Star looked on indulgently. "Heather's just kidding. We wouldn't go on this trip without Emily."

A tall, handsome man came along the boardwalk and hopped up the café steps. His brown eyes crinkled as they met Jenny's. He bent down to kiss his wife and child.

Jenny settled into her husband's arms, her mouth stretched in a wide smile.

Jenny had been a suburban soccer mom for most of her life, until her ex-husband traded her in for a younger model. She had accepted her aunt's invitation and sought shelter in Pelican Cove, a remote barrier island off the coast of Virginia. Jenny's life had taken a sharp turn after that. She had thrived as a local café owner, churning out delectable treats for locals and tourists alike. Her delicious food had helped the town flourish, and people flocked to Pelican Cove from far and wide just to visit the Boardwalk Café.

Jenny's personal life had been a roller coaster ride. Wooed by two handsome men, she had made a disastrous choice. Her fateful trip to the altar had turned out to be a big surprise. She was now married to Jason Stone, the local lawyer and her best friend. She was helping him raise his daughter Emily who was almost a year old.

"Are you ladies going on a trip?" Jason asked.

"We are all going," Molly Henderson said eagerly.

Tall and scrawny, she wore thick Coke bottle glasses and worked at the local library.

"Chris is coming too. So it's not just a ladies' trip. You have no excuses this time, Jason."

"I'm not making any, Molly," Jason told her. "My work load is light for a change and it's finally spring. We all need a change after that grueling winter."

"Let's talk about possible locations," Star said.

"What about the Blue Ridge Mountains?" Betty Sue asked. "I have never been there and I hear they are very pretty in the spring."

Everyone plunged in, going back and forth with their suggestions until Molly stood up to go back to work. That broke the group up and they agreed to finalize their plans when they met the next day.

"I can't believe the Magnolias are going on a trip," Jenny gushed as she mixed strawberry chicken salad for lunch.

Magnolias was the moniker the women had given themselves, based on Heather's favorite movie.

"Don't forget Jason and Chris are coming too," Star said, stirring tomato soup on the stove.

Star was a local artist who painted seascapes of the surrounding region. She often helped Jenny at the café.

The lunch crowd started streaming in. A lively trio burst into the café, talking their heads off about some movie star. Jenny recognized the voices and went out to greet them.

A tall, blonde girl sprang up with a squeal and wrapped Jenny in a tight hug.

"How's my favorite café owner?" she asked.

"How's my favorite highschooler?" Jenny asked lovingly as she patted the girl on her back.

"I'm going to college in the fall, Jenny," the girl preened. "I got two acceptance letters already. But Daddy wants me to go to UVA because that's his alma mater."

"That's a thing with dads," Jenny told her. "My Nick went to Georgetown because his father went there."

The short, cherubic young man accompanying the pretty girl cleared his throat. The café chair creaked under his weight. Jenny figured he easily weighed three hundred pounds.

"Tell her why we are here, Bella!"

"Oh, right, I almost forgot," Isabella Worthington said, slapping her head. "I am having a secret party, Jenny. And you just have to cater it."

"What's secret about it?" Jenny asked, quirking an eyebrow. "Nothing I wouldn't do?"

The plump girl with a mouth full of braces laughed out loud.

"Shut up, Ashley," Bella said. "You have nothing to worry about, Jenny. It's going to be the best party anyone ever threw in Pelican Cove."

"It's going to be lit," the boy bobbed his head up and down, his eyes gleaming with excitement.

"Forget about the party for a while," Ashley complained. "I'm starving."

Jenny brought out a tray loaded with tomato soup and chicken salad sandwiches.

"Save room for dessert. I have triple chocolate brownies."

"Sam's tongue is hanging out," Bella sniggered and

high fived Ashley.

Sam ignored her and looked at Jenny.

"I am going to need two more sandwiches."

"Why don't you finish everything on your plate first?" Jenny asked kindly.

"Sam will scarf all that down in minutes," Bella laughed. "He just eats a lot, Jenny."

Jenny went in to get more sandwiches, marveling at youthful appetites.

"So you're doing my party, right?" Bella asked, taking a dainty bite of her sandwich.

Large diamond studs sparkled in her ears, matching the big solitaire that hung around her neck on a thin gold chain. The red soles of her shoes hinted at a pricey designer label. Jenny was sure the casual clothes she wore cost three figures. Isabella Worthington had plenty of money and she believed in splurging it at every possible opportunity. But she had a heart of gold.

Her friends were obviously not as well off as her. The girl Ashley had done a poor job of imitating Bella. Jenny barely remembered her high school days but she knew girls tried to ape the popular girl. Ashley's clothes came off super market hangers, although they tried to copy the same fashions Bella wore. Ashley just looked like a cheaper, poorer version of Bella.

Jenny had catered a holiday party for the Worthingtons the previous winter. She had immediately taken to the effusive young motherless girl who was like a princess in a castle. Bella had become a regular at the Boardwalk Café and she frequently dragged in some of her friends along with her.

"I have never catered a party for teenagers," Jenny admitted. "What are you kids eating these days?"

"Whatever you cook, make sure there's lots of it," Sam spoke with his mouth full. "We don't want to run out."

"Jenny always has plenty of food," Bella said right away. "I don't know, Jenny. Something fun, like burgers or Sloppy Joes?"

"Aren't you too old for Sloppy Joes?" Jenny teased. "You are almost 21, aren't you?"

"I will be turning twenty in a few weeks," Bella said proudly. "Sam here is already 21."

"He got held back," Ashley said suddenly.

Sam turned red and finally stopped eating. He glared at Ashley with a malevolent expression.

"Stop it, you two," Bella quipped. She turned toward

Jenny. "Why don't you give me a few ideas, Jenny? We can finalize the menu later."

"I'm going on a small trip this weekend," Jenny told Bella.

Bella's lips curved into a smile as she heard about the spring vistas in the Blue Ridge Mountains. She looked at her friends and they yelled in unison.

"Road trip!"

"We are coming with you, Jenny," Bella declared. "Don't worry about a thing."

"I need to discuss this with my friends," Jenny reminded her.

She wasn't sure the others would want some kids tagging along with them.

"You have a baby with you, and that museum piece," Bella said, referring to Betty Sue. "You need some young blood. We'll show you how to have a good time."

"Don't get carried away just yet, Bella," Jenny warned. "I still need to talk to the others."

Bella acted as if she hadn't heard Jenny.

"We are going to have a great time. I'm gonna make

sure of that."

Bella and her friends skipped out of the café, already planning a shopping spree before the road trip.

Jenny broached the topic with the Magnolias the next day.

"That Bella Worthington is one spoilt brat," Betty Sue spat, putting her knitting down. "But she's sweet."

"Are you actually saying yes, Grandma?" Heather asked, surprised.

"The more, the merrier," Betty Sue said with a shrug. "Let those kids tag along. But it's going to be your job to keep them in line, Jenny."

"Don't worry, Betty Sue," Jenny assured her. "I will make sure they behave."

Heather and Molly planned an elaborate trip. Bella pulled some strings and got them rooms at a swanky resort at half off. Jenny and Star baked several batches of cookies to take along with them.

The big day arrived. Everyone had decided to assemble at the Boardwalk Café. Jenny and her friends stood outside, waiting for Bella to turn up. Betty Sue started getting impatient after five minutes.

"When did being on time go out of fashion?" she

grumbled.

They heard a loud honk just then. Jason let out a low whistle and Jenny's mouth dropped open as a stretch limo as long as a block slowly ambled onto their street. Bella and Ashley were hanging out of the sun roof, sipping bubbly drinks from tall flutes.

"That better not be champagne," Jenny muttered.

Bella let out a whoop as soon as the car stopped in front of the café.

"What's all this?" Heather asked, getting caught up in the excitement.

"We are traveling in style," Bella announced. "All the ladies can fit in easily. There's a wet bar with champagne and caviar."

"We can't afford all this, honey," Star said frankly. "We don't have a rich Daddy."

"You don't need to pay anything," Bella said with a smug smile. "It's all on me."

"Bella!" Jenny exclaimed. "Are you sure? This car must have cost a fortune."

"Don't worry about it, Jenny," Bella assured her. "It's just a little something I'm doing for my friends. Just have a good time, okay."

The Magnolias grudgingly gave in and piled into the luxurious car. Sam was already inside, sprawled over a couple of seats. Jason and Chris followed in his car, with Emily strapped in her seat in the back.

Jason wondered how Max Worthington would react to his daughter's extravagance.

Chapter 2

The Magnolias returned to Pelican Cove with wide smiles on their faces.

Jenny and Heather were having a planning session on the deck of the Boardwalk Café. Jenny needed to plan the spring specials for the café menu. Heather was helping her choose the most popular dishes based on what people had liked on social media.

"Start making your shrimp po'boys again," Heather told her. "And how about something sweet?"

"We are already selling cupcakes and truffles. But as the weather warms up, people go to the Creamery for their ice cream." Jenny observed.

"You got it, Jenny," Heather beamed. "You need to start serving frozen desserts."

"But the Creamery makes the best ice cream in Pelican Cove," Jenny objected. "I can't top that."

"That's it," Heather burst out. "You can top it.

"Heather, you are making no sense!"

"Take the ice cream from the Creamery and make it

better. I'm sure you can do it, Jenny. You are so innovative."

"You mean like an ice cream sundae?" Jenny asked with a frown.

"Exactly! I'm sure you can come up with yummy toppings like your salted caramel or that hot fudge you make."

"We can have hot fudge sundaes," Jenny said eagerly, as her mind began whirling with ideas. "With toasted almonds. And caramel sundaes with walnuts, like a turtle ice cream. Something with strawberries, and something with pineapple and toasted coconut …"

"Whoa!" Heather laughed. "You're on a roll, Jenny. But you get the idea. I'm sure the people are going to love them."

"I'll start working on some recipes soon," Jenny promised. "Get ready to taste them later this week."

"I will never say no to ice cream," Heather sighed dramatically, placing a hand on her heart.

"Maybe I can offer free samples," Jenny thought out loud.

"Why don't you call Bella and her friends?" Heather asked. "Get the young people's opinion."

"That's an excellent idea, Heather!" Jenny approved. "She must be exhausted after her party."

"Probably still hung over," Heather rolled her eyes.

"No way," Jenny said, shaking her head. "Bella's not into that kind of stuff."

"Kids will be kids, Jenny."

"How can you say that, after all she did for us?"

"So she splurged on a limo," Heather shrugged. "She's a spoilt brat. Rich spoilt brat. She would've squandered the money anyhow. If not on us, on something else."

"Are you denying you had a good time?" Jenny asked irately, her hands on her hips.

"I had the best time!" Heather nodded. "This trip to the Blue Ridge Mountains was epic. But I don't think that young minx had anything to do with it."

"You're prejudiced," Jenny said with a grimace. "I don't know why."

"Bella Worthington's a bit over the top for me," Heather declared. "She's been indulged too much, if you ask me."

"Maybe her father's trying to make up for being a single parent," Jenny offered.

Heather had lost both her parents in a car accident when she was a teen.

"My Grandma didn't spoil me," she scoffed. She drummed her fingers on the table for a minute, staring at the turquoise ocean. "My God, Jenny," she burst out. "Do you think I'm jealous of her?"

Jenny patted Heather on the back.

"Maybe a little. But I don't blame you. Bella seems to lead a charming life. I'm sure plenty of people envy her."

Star came out on the deck.

"Time for coffee. Are you two done yet?"

"I wonder what's holding Grandma up," Heather said. She stood up and walked to the edge of the deck, scanning the beach for any sign of Betty Sue. "There she is," Heather said with relief. "Why is she bringing Tootsie along?"

Tootsie was Heather's black poodle and Jenny hadn't seen a pet who was more pampered.

Betty Sue was red in the face by the time she reached the café. She handed over Tootsie's leash to Heather and collapsed in a chair. Her eyes were as red as her face and it looked like she had been crying.

"What's the matter, Grandma?" Heather exclaimed. "Are you feeling unwell?"

Betty Sue pulled out a lace handkerchief and dabbed at her eyes. She was so overcome with emotion she couldn't speak a word. Jenny poured a cup of coffee and added cream and plenty of sugar. She thrust the cup toward Betty Sue.

"Drink this."

Betty Sue's hands shook as she gratefully accepted the cup. She took a couple of sips and dissolved into tears again.

"You're scaring me now, Grandma!" Heather cried. "What's the matter with you?"

"It's that child," Betty Sue said with a sob. "Bella. She's dead."

Jenny's eyes grew wide and her mouth hung open. Heather's reaction was something similar.

"Have you been dipping in the brandy, Betty Sue?" Star asked scornfully. "What's this nonsense you are spouting?"

"It's all over town," Betty Sue said, shaking her head. "That poor girl."

"Why don't you tell us everything from the

beginning?" Jenny suggested.

She felt a heavy weight on her chest and her hand clutched the chair she was sitting in. She hoped Betty Sue was mistaken.

"Bella was in a car accident last night," Betty Sue told them. "She was gone by the time the paramedics got to her."

"Wasn't the party last night?" Heather asked, hugging Tootsie tighter.

The poodle squirmed out of her grasp and jumped down. Tootsie wasn't usually allowed in the café and Heather tied her up near the café steps. But Jenny was too shocked to notice.

"I delivered all their food around five," Jenny whispered. "Bella thanked me with one of her signature hugs."

"She must have been going home from the party," Betty Sue shrugged.

"Wait a minute," Heather said. "So Bella's party wasn't in her own home?"

"It was in someone's basement," Jenny explained.

Star had been rooted to a spot in shock. She finally seemed to snap awake.

"I don't believe this. I'm going to call up a few people and make sure Betty Sue got it right."

She was back a few minutes later, the look on her face clearly indicating what she had found.

"She was a sweet girl," Betty Sue said mournfully. "Too young to be taken from us."

"What about the other driver?" Heather asked suddenly. "I guess she hit someone?"

"Wrapped the car around a tree," Betty Sue said. "People are saying she lost control."

"Why?" Heather asked. "Was she drunk?"

"You don't know that, Heather," Jenny reprimanded her. "This is how rumors get started."

"It was just a question," Heather said lamely. "Maybe she had a flat."

Jenny's eyes filled up as the news finally hit her. She stared at the water and tried to make sense of what she had heard. Not that accidents ever made sense. She spotted Jason hurrying along the boardwalk. He leapt up the stairs and rushed toward Jenny.

"So you've heard," he said as soon as he saw her tear stained face.

He hugged Jenny tightly and began stroking her back. Seeing Jason unlocked another well of emotion in Jenny and she sobbed into his shoulder.

"I don't believe him," Jason said. "Kid's just trying to get some attention."

Jenny wiped her eyes with her hands and stared uncomprehendingly at Jason.

"What are you talking about, Jason?"

"So you don't know," Jason sighed. "Kid called Calvin Butler is kicking up a storm. Says Bella was murdered."

"Murdered!" Jenny gasped. "But Betty Sue just said she had an accident."

"This Calvin guy witnessed the whole thing. He says it was murder. He is challenging the authorities. Everyone is waiting for the autopsy results now."

"But why would anyone want to murder Bella!" Jenny gasped. "And how? Did someone tamper with her car?"

"I don't know much," Jason admitted. "It's all just speculation at this point. The police are not saying much."

Jason went back to his office for an appointment. Jenny spent the rest of the day in a daze. Bella's pretty

blue eyes and smiling face kept flashing before her.
Her laughter rang in her ears. Jenny thought about all
the fun they had at the resort in the mountains. Bella
had been a normal teenager, full of life and looking
forward to her future.

The café was packed with a crowd of people who had
come out of their homes to catch the latest gossip. It
seemed like everywhere Jenny turned, people were
talking about Bella. She sighed with relief when she
could finally shut the café and head home.

Jenny lived in a three storied sea facing mansion called
Seaview. Her aunt Star lived with her and Star's special
friend Jimmy Parsons was a frequent visitor. Jason and
Emily had moved in after the wedding. With Jenny and
Jason both busy during the day, they had finally given
in and hired a full time nanny for the baby. She was a
local and came highly recommended by Jason's aunt.
Luckily, Emily took to the gentle older woman right
away.

Jenny had converted one of the rooms on the second
floor into a nursery. Although they hadn't decorated it
yet, it held a crib and a stack of shelves for housing
Emily's toys. Emily was down for a nap when Jenny
looked in on her. She went to her own room and
collapsed on her bed. Her eyes shut of their own
accord and the fluttering curtains were casting long
shadows when she woke up a couple of hours later.
Jason had an appointment in the city and wasn't

expected back until later.

Jenny stifled a yawn and trudged down the steps to the kitchen. She poured herself some juice and sipped it slowly as she watched the sun set over the horizon from her kitchen window.

Star was out in the living room, playing with Emily.

Jenny started chopping some vegetables for dinner, planning to make a pot of chili. The doorbell rang, interrupting her. Star came in, bouncing Emily in her arms.

"Someone for you," she said, shrugging her shoulders at Jenny's questioning glance.

Jenny pulled off her apron and went outside.

A short, skinny boy sat on the edge of the couch. His face was pockmarked with severe acne and his thick black glasses matched his hair. He wore neatly pressed khaki trousers and a shirt with the top button done.

The boy stood up when he saw Jenny and licked his lips nervously.

"My name is Calvin Butler," he said, offering a hand.

Jenny thought the name sounded familiar but she didn't make the connection right away.

"How can I help you?"

"I am here for Bella," the boy said, biting a nail.

Jenny noticed it was full of grime.

"Bella," Jenny whispered. She realized who he was. "Why do you think Bella was murdered?" she asked.

The boy's composure slipped.

"I am telling you she was. And I know who did it too. It was that cheapo friend of hers, Ashley Burns."

"You are saying Ashley killed Bella?" Jenny asked bewildered. "How is that possible? I heard Bella was in a car accident."

The boy's glasses slid down his nose. He pushed them back with force and scowled at Jenny.

"Ashley was driving the car. She lived. Bella didn't."

"Why would Ashley want to harm Bella?" Jenny asked, her hands on her hips.

"Ashley hated Bella," Calvin declared. "She wanted Bella's life. She tried to copy everything Bella did and failed miserably. But I never thought she would go so far."

"Why are you getting involved?" Jenny asked him.

"Bella meant a lot to me," Calvin said. "I'm going to make sure her killer doesn't roam free."

Jenny folded her hands and looked down on the boy.

"I loved Bella too. I will look into this but let me warn you. My goal is to find out what really happened. If you had anything to do with this, I won't be doing you any favors."

Chapter 3

Jenny was curious about the car Bella had lost her life in. Would the car provide some clue to why Ashley had lost control of the vehicle? Jenny was used to pumping her ex Adam for information. Adam was the local sheriff and very particular about not mixing his professional life with his private. But Jenny's persistence had always yielded her some tidbit. Since talking to Adam wasn't an option, Jenny decided she would just have to be more resourceful.

Calvin Butler had told Jenny where they had taken the vehicle Bella had been in. Jenny had no idea how he had obtained that information. She also wasn't sure if she could believe him. But she figured there was only one way to find out.

Jenny packed a couple of ham and grilled pineapple sandwiches along with some cookies. She added a bottle of her fresh brewed sweet tea. She hoped it would be enough to soften the toughest gatekeeper at the local impound.

Heather stood watching her with a skeptical expression.

"Are you planning to bribe the guard with your food?"

"Something like that," Jenny agreed.

"You know I love anything you cook, Jenny, but that's a bit ambitious, isn't it?"

"Are you coming with me or not?" Jenny demanded, lugging the basket and heading out.

"Of course I'm coming." Heather followed Jenny out to her car.

They reached the local car impound five minutes later. A stout man in a policeman's uniform sat in a booth guarding a padlocked gate. Barbed wire fence cordoned off a lot full of all kinds of vehicles. Many of them looked like they had been there for years, covered in a thick layer of dirt.

"We need to get inside," Heather declared before Jenny had a chance to greet the man.

The man looked bored. He held his hand out expectantly and groused.

"You got a receipt?"

"We just want to look around," Heather said, shaking her head.

"Sorry lady, you can't get in without a receipt."

Heather gave the man a withering look.

"What do you think we are gonna do? Drive one of these rust buckets out of here?"

The man shook his head and went back to solving his crossword puzzle.

Jenny elbowed Heather out of the way and stepped up to the cabin. She cleared her throat and stretched her mouth into a smile.

"It must be awful hard work," she noted, "sitting here all day with no one to talk to."

The man looked up and scratched his head.

"You get used to it," he said with a shrug.

"Have you had lunch yet?" Jenny asked. "I was taking this lunch basket over to a friend but she's not home."

"I bring my own lunch," the man grumbled. "The missus packs a baloney sandwich for me every day."

Jenny's face fell. The man's expression softened a bit.

"What you got there, lady?"

"Just a ham and pineapple sandwich with Dijon mustard and arugula," Jenny said.

"Aru … what? Sounds weird. I'm a meat and potatoes man."

"It's just lettuce with a fancy name," Jenny said with a laugh. "Just give it a shot."

"Jenny's a great cook," Heather joined in. "Folks come from up and down the coast to eat her food."

"There's chocolate chip cookies in there too," Jenny said, hefting the basket and placing it on the counter.

Any resolve the man may have had collapsed when he spotted the cookies.

"Thank you kindly," he said. "Guess I'm having a fancy lunch today. Wait till the missus hears about this."

"You are welcome," Jenny said. "I can get the basket from you some other time."

The man craned his neck and looked right and left. He beckoned Jenny closer.

"What's in that parking lot, lady?"

Jenny thought on her feet.

"I heard some of these cars are coming up for auction later this month. I just wanted to take a peek and see if there are any worth bidding for."

"Most of them are clunkers," the man dismissed. "Look, I'll let you in just this once. But this stays between us."

"I'm not gonna blab," Jenny promised.

The man pulled a set of keys off a peg and climbed down from his perch. He stepped out of the booth and unlocked the gate, ushering Jenny and Heather inside. He locked the gate after them, promising to open it when they were ready to leave.

"That was a master stroke, Jenny," Heather giggled. "You had him eating out of your hand."

"Shhh ..." Jenny cautioned her. "You gather more flies with honey. Remember that, Heather."

They walked through a couple of rows. Almost every car they saw looked like it had been there for months.

"How are you going to spot Bella's car?" Heather asked. "Do you know what it looks like?"

"It's actually Ashley's car. Calvin said it's a yellow Beetle. That should be easy to spot."

"There it is!" Heather exclaimed, pointing toward a bright car at the end of the lot.

Jenny cried out in dismay when they reached the car. The front fender had crumpled completely on the right side. The windshield was shattered and a few bits of glass still littered the car floor. Heather and Jenny clutched each other's hands as they took in the battered car.

"I can barely look at it," Heather said with a shudder.

"Same here," Jenny agreed, pulling her phone out of her bag.

She began taking pictures of the car from different angles. She moved closer to the passenger seat in the front and tried to take photos of the interior.

"Did you see this, Heather?" she asked suddenly. "The seat belt's broken."

Heather walked to her side and forced herself to look inside the car.

"You're right, Jenny. Bella was in this seat, wasn't she?"

The girls shared a grim look.

"I think I've taken enough photos," Jenny said. "Let's go now."

They hurried out of the lot and waited quietly while the guard let them out. He was full of praise for Jenny's food. Jenny took the empty basket from him and thanked him again.

The girls were quiet on their way back to the café.

Heather finally broke the silence.

"Poor Bella! Do you want to cancel our plans for tonight, Jenny? I am sure Molly won't mind."

"We are definitely meeting tonight," Jenny said. "I need a night with my special girls."

Jenny handled the café crowd and prepped for the next day. She was exhausted by the time she got into her car to drive home. She had kept a tight lid on her emotions all day but she finally allowed a few tears to trickle down. Bella's laughter rang in her ears again and she resolved to find out what had happened. Had Bella's death just been an accident or was there any substance to Calvin's claims?

Emily's chatter reached Jenny before she went in through her front door. Jenny immediately felt lighter. Star was in the living room with her friend Jimmy. Emily was playing with her toys in her pen.

"You look done in," Star observed. "How about a cup of chamomile tea?"

Jenny collapsed on a couch and let her aunt pamper her.

"Just put your feet up and relax, sweetie," Star said gently. "I already got the snacks for tonight. I made crab dip and pimento cheese. Lasagna's in the oven. Molly's getting brownies and Heather's making strawberry daiquiris when she gets here. You don't worry about a thing."

"You spoil me rotten," Jenny sighed.

Emily extended her arms toward Jenny and started to babble, trying to stand up. Star pulled her out of the playpen and deposited her in Jenny's lap. The child snuggled close to Jenny and began sucking on her thumb.

"I missed you too, baby," Jenny said, planting a bunch of kisses all over her head.

Heather, Molly and Betty Sue arrived a few minutes later.

"I think that's my cue to leave," Jimmy said, getting up. "Have fun, ladies. And be good."

Emily's nanny took her up to the nursery.

The Magnolias each settled into their favorite seats in Jenny's living room. Heather and Molly sat on fat cushions on the carpet. Star and Betty Sue had picked an armchair each. Jenny reclined on a couch, unable to shake off her melancholy mood.

"How's married life with Jason?" Heather asked. "Doesn't it feel weird? Being in a loveless marriage?"

"Jason loves her," Molly reminded them. "He's always

had a thing for Jenny."

"We never got to talk about this," Heather said bluntly. "What prompted you to say yes when Jason proposed at the altar?"

Molly's eyes widened. She stole a glance at Jenny, expecting her to fly off the handle. But Jenny didn't seem bothered by the question.

"I have asked myself that a hundred times since that day," she admitted. "I always knew Jason was in love with me. He told me that several times. But I surprised myself by saying yes."

"Why did you choose to date Adam over Jason?" Molly asked softly.

"I'm not sure," Jenny told her. "I thought he needed me more."

"What about love? Do you think he stopped loving you?" Molly pressed.

"Adam's always been unpredictable," Jenny said. "I have no idea what went wrong that day, why he didn't turn up at the wedding. And I don't know if I will ever find out. I'm not sure I want to. Adam and I are done."

"I think that's the right attitude, girl," Betty Sue said. "You have a bright future ahead of you with your new husband."

"Do you really think of Jason as your husband?" Heather probed.

"He's more of a friend right now," Jenny admitted. "But he's my best friend. I do love him, you know. I'm just not in love with him yet."

"What does that even mean?" Heather cried out, frustrated. "It doesn't make any sense."

"Simmer down, Heather," Betty Sue snapped. "It's beyond your grasp."

"That's exactly why I want to understand," Heather pouted.

"Look, I don't have all the answers," Jenny said. "You know how devastated I was when Adam didn't turn up for the wedding. I felt like a big fool, standing there in my wedding dress, clutching my bridal bouquet. Then Jason got down on one knee and declared his undying love. He promised to keep me happy for the rest of my life. Something strange happened to me in that moment. I felt this warm and fuzzy glow inside me, like my heart would melt. I felt I could trust Jason. I believed he would never let me down."

"But you didn't have to marry him right then," Heather said, incensed. "Are you even compatible?"

"We have the rest of our lives to find that out," Jenny said. "I trust Jason will do anything to make me happy. I want to do the same for him. He is a man of integrity and has a kind heart. That's not a bad foundation for a marriage."

"Hear, hear," Star said, holding aloft her glass in a toast.

"I say you are going to be madly in love with Jason before this year is out," Molly said. "Remember I called it."

"What about Emily?" Heather asked. "Are you ready to be a mother at your age?"

"Emily's the cherry on the cake," Jenny said. "She's my little princess."

"You're one of a kind, Jenny," Heather laughed. "I hope you and Jason get your happily ever after."

"We are living our happily ever after right now," Jenny said brightly, and realized she meant every word.

Her life had taken an unexpected turn but she had found joy beyond her wildest dreams behind it.

Chapter 4

Pelican Cove was experiencing a bright spring day. Jenny hummed a tune as she stirred a pot of caramel at the cafe. The breakfast rush was over and she was waiting for the Magnolias to come in for their coffee break.

Betty Sue arrived, lugging a large tote bag bursting with three colors of wool. Heather was right behind her, tapping keys on her phone.

"Something smells good," she said, taking a deep breath.

"Caramel for my salted caramel sundaes," Jenny told her. "I'm trying to get it just right."

Molly and Star arrived and the women got busy talking about the latest happenings in Pelican Cove.

"Ashley's mother came in yesterday," Molly told them. "Checked out a bunch of her favorite books. Poor girl is still laid up in hospital, you know."

"What's poor about her?" Heather scoffed. "She's still alive, isn't she? That's more than I can say for Bella."

"She's a victim too, Heather," Jenny protested.

"We don't know that. She was driving, wasn't she? I say she is responsible for that accident."

"Why don't you go and talk to her?" Star suggested. "Get the story from the horse's mouth."

"That's a great idea," Jenny said. "Want to go with me, Heather?"

"Wait a minute," Betty Sue said, looking up from her knitting. "Didn't I hear something about caramel?"

"It's not perfect yet," Jenny said. "I'm trying to make it bitter without burning it."

Jenny packed a basket of fresh muffins and three types of cookies to take with her to the hospital. Heather tagged along, rolling her eyes when Jenny stopped at the gift shop to get some fresh flowers for Ashley.

Ashley's appearance shocked them when they entered her hospital room. There was a big brace around her neck, her arm was in a sling and there was a cast on her leg. Her face brightened when she saw Jenny.

"How are you doing, Ashley?" Jenny asked, her voice full of concern. "You look like you are in a lot of pain."

"They gave me a bunch of painkillers so it's not too bad." Ashley gave them a watery smile.

Jenny looked around for an empty vase to put the flowers in. She spotted a picture frame on the little table next to Ashley's bed. It was a group photo with Ashley and Bella dressed in pretty dresses in the middle and some boys wearing tuxedos flanking them. Jenny spotted Sam right away. She had to lean closer to recognize one of them as Calvin.

"That was taken at our junior prom last year," Ashley said wistfully. "Bella was the prom queen, of course."

Jenny thought she detected a hint of bitterness in Ashley's voice.

"So how did you get in this mess, Ashley?" Heather asked, jumping in. "Something was wrong with the car?"

Jenny pulled at Heather's arm, warning her to slow down but the damage was done. Tears welled up in Ashley's eyes.

"It's my fault," she cried. "It's all my fault. I can't believe she's gone."

"Didn't your car have an airbag?" Jenny asked.

"Only at the driver's side," Ashley told them. "It was an old car. It's all my parents could afford. Not like Bella's fancy Mercedes."

"Bella shouldn't have got into your jalopy, I guess,"

Heather snorted.

"She shouldn't have," Ashley agreed. "We took her car whenever we went out but her car was in the garage that day so we were using mine." Her voice broke again. "Bella's gone because of me."

Jenny surmised Ashley was feeling survivor's guilt.

"You should focus on getting better now, Ashley," she said gently.

Ashley sobbed uncontrollably. "Bella was so happy that day."

"How was the party?" Jenny asked. "I have no idea what kids do for fun these days."

"Just the usual, you know," Ashley told them. "Loud music, junk food and a keg or two. Except we had really great food because of you, Jenny."

"You had alcohol at this party?" Jenny asked, trying not to sound judgmental.

She needed to keep it light if she wanted to get some information out of Ashley.

"It wouldn't be a party without booze," Ashley said frankly.

"Aren't you and Bella underage?" Heather pounced.

Ashley's face settled in a pout.

"You're not her mom, Heather," Jenny said. She turned toward Ashley, hoping the girl wasn't going to clam up. "Looks like you had plenty of fun at this party."

"It was one of the best we've had this year," Ashley nodded. "And then that thing about Bella and Jake ... Bella's so lucky. She gets what she wants every time."

"What about Bella and Jake?"

Jenny knew Jake was Bella's boyfriend. She had talked about him nonstop when they went on their trip to the mountains.

"They got engaged," Ashley said with a sigh. "It was supposed to be a secret."

"What?" Jenny exclaimed. "Did her family know about this?"

"Bella's Dad didn't approve of Jake. He's a deadbeat, you know. Dropped out of school a couple of years ago. Just hangs around the docks doing nothing."

"What was the rush?" Heather asked. "Wasn't she just a teenager?"

"She was going to be twenty next month," Ashley reminded them. "Bella said they would get married as soon as she graduated."

"Did Bella have a lot to drink at the party?" Jenny asked. "Is that why you were dropping her home?"

"We both had a few drinks," Ashley admitted.

"So you weren't the designated driver," Heather muttered.

"I always drove Bella everywhere," Ashley said, her eyes tearing up again. "She didn't have her driving permit. Never passed the test. She was deathly afraid of getting behind the wheel of a car."

"So you knew you were going to drive Bella home," Heather hounded Ashley. "Yet you guzzled beer at that party? Don't you think that was highly irresponsible?"

"Calm down, Heather," Jenny urged. "Can't you see she's sorry?"

"That's not going to bring Bella back!" Heather exclaimed, glaring at Ashley. "Do your parents know about this? What else did you do at that party? Smoke pot? Or something worse than that!"

Ashley's face had crumpled and tears streamed down her face again.

"I'm sorry, I'm sorry," she sobbed. "Bella was so

popular! She could drink beer like nobody's business. I just wanted to be like her. I wanted everyone to like me too."

Jenny tried to console the poor girl without any success. A nurse heard the commotion and came in. She took one look at Ashley and shooed them out.

"We didn't get much out of her," Heather said as they got into Jenny's car.

"You were really hard on her," Jenny noted. "What's the matter with you, Heather?"

"I'm not the villain here, Jenny," Heather argued. "That girl was drunk and driving under the influence. No wonder she crashed that car. She needs to own up to it."

"Didn't you see she's full of remorse?" Jenny asked. "I don't think she's getting over this any time soon."

"I say she got off easy," Heather huffed, banging her fist into the door.

Jenny wondered why Heather was so unsettled. Her phone rang before she could ask her about it. Jenny listened for a few minutes and hung up, promising to be there soon.

"That was the nanny," she told Heather. "The baby won't stop crying. We need to go home."

"Let's hurry, Jenny," Heather nodded.

Jenny tried to drive quickly without breaking the speed limit. They pulled up at Seaview fifteen minutes later. Jenny rushed in and pulled a crying Emily out of her play pen and into her arms.

The nanny looked relieved.

"She's been crying nonstop for the past hour. I tried everything. I played her favorite music, gave her all her toys, even took her out in the garden. She just won't stop."

Jenny stroked the baby's back and tried to calm her down. Emily whimpered for a bit and started howling again.

"Is she sick?" Heather asked. "Let's take her to a doctor."

"Why didn't I think of that?" Jenny wailed. "Can you drive, please? I'm a bundle of nerves."

They were back at the hospital and in the emergency room a few minutes later. Heather spotted a nurse she knew and convinced her to fast track them. The doctor pronounced that Emily had an ear infection. Soon, Emily was sleeping peacefully in Jenny's arms. By the time Heather drove them back home, Jenny was exhausted. The nanny took the baby to her nursery and Jenny collapsed on the couch in her living room.

Star woke her up an hour later, carrying a bowl of hot soup.

"Why don't you eat something? You look done in."

"How did things go at the café?" Jenny asked. "I am so sorry I deserted you."

"I can handle the café, Jenny. You needed to be here."

"What am I doing, Star?" Jenny asked. "Am I cut out to be a mother?"

"You raised a fine young man," Star reminded her. "You're a great mom, Jenny."

"But that was years ago. Am I too old for this?"

"Where's this coming from?" Star asked, sitting down next to Jenny. "It's not like you to doubt yourself so much."

"Emily scared me today," Jenny admitted. "She was inconsolable. I couldn't tell what was wrong with her."

"You took quick action," Star told her. "I think you couldn't have done better."

"I hope Jason gets home soon," Jenny said. "I'm responsible for Emily in his absence."

"He trusts you, Jenny," Star said, patting her on the

back. "You need to trust yourself more."

Jenny flew into Jason's arms the minute he got home that evening. He had been away in the city.

"I'm so glad you're back," Jenny sobbed into his shoulder.

Jason took her hand and went up to the nursery. Emily was awake in her nanny's arms and guzzling milk from her bottle.

"She looks fine to me," he said to his wife.

"You weren't here earlier. She must have been in a lot of pain."

"I'm glad she's better now."

"I'm so sorry, Jason," Jenny said.

"What are you apologizing for?" Jason laughed. "She's a baby. She's going to get sick."

"She scared me," Jenny admitted. "You weren't here. I wasn't sure I was doing right by her."

"I've never met anyone more caring than you, Jenny," Jason said. "I have faith in you. You are the best mommy my baby girl could have."

"I'd forgotten how hard it is to see your baby cry,"

Jenny admitted. "My heart was in my mouth the whole time we were at the hospital."

"I'm sorry I wasn't there with you," Jason told her. "But you handled everything admirably, Jenny. You must be exhausted."

"It's been a long day," Jenny nodded, stifling a yawn.

"Why don't I pour us some wine?" Jason asked. "Let's build a fire in the living room and take our plates out there."

"Star went out with Jimmy," Jenny told him. "I'm afraid I haven't had a chance to cook any dinner for us."

"I took care of that, honey." Jason gave her a knowing smile.

"Chinese food from the city?" Jenny squealed. "I've been craving Chinese food all week."

Jenny reclined on her couch in front of a roaring fire. Jason sat with an arm around her, gazing adoringly into her eyes. Jenny sipped her wine and crossed her fingers behind her back, marveling at her new life.

Chapter 5

"How's my favorite café owner?" Jason asked, peeking into the kitchen at the Boardwalk Café the next morning.

Jenny's face broke into a smile. She poured spiced strawberry syrup over a stack of pancakes and added some whipped cream on top. The middle of the week meant the café wasn't bursting at the seams with tourists. But her regulars still wanted breakfast. Jenny had started offering breakfast specials at half off on Wednesdays and they were an instant hit.

"What are you doing here, Jason?" she asked.

"My 9 AM cancelled at the last moment," he told her. "I thought I would get a hot breakfast."

He patted his stomach and looked longingly at the plate in Jenny's hands.

"These are not for you, but I will fix you some in a minute," Jenny promised.

Star arrived just then and convinced Jenny to take a break.

"Go have some breakfast with your husband. All these

chores will still be here when you are done."

Jenny pushed some eggs around her plate while Jason devoured his pancakes. He finally put his knife and fork down and took a sip of his coffee.

"You can start talking now," Jenny said, leaning forward.

"Nothing gets past you, Jenny," Jason said, his eyes shining with admiration.

"Let's just say you are not good at hiding stuff from me," Jenny smiled.

Jason's brow furrowed as he wiped his mouth with a napkin.

"The police are charging Ashley for Bella's death," he told her. "Her parents hired me this morning."

"Is it because she was driving under the influence?" Jenny asked. "Poor girl."

"You really feel sorry for her?" Jason asked, surprised. "What about Bella?"

"I don't think Ashley did it on purpose. It was an accident. But I agree she shouldn't have been drinking and driving."

"Her parents are devastated. They can't believe their

girl drank at that party."

Jenny's son had been a teenager not long ago. She knew it was hard to keep a constant watch on kids that age.

"We need to find out more about this party," Jenny mused. "I am going to talk to Calvin again."

Jason left for his office and Jenny placed a call to Calvin Butler. He agreed to meet her at his home. Jenny decided to go and talk to him right away.

Calvin was dressed in another pair of neatly pressed khakis and a shirt that was tightly buttoned at the throat. He licked his lips nervously as he greeted Jenny. Jenny decided Calvin was a handsome boy under all the welts and scars.

Jenny walked through a well appointed living room into an open kitchen.

"Where are your parents?" she asked.

"They both work in the city and get back late," Calvin told her. "I'm on my own pretty much all the time."

"I wanted to talk to you about Bella's party," Jenny began. "Were you there that day?"

Calvin pulled out a folding knife out of his pocket and began slicing an apple. He arranged the slices on a small crystal plate and offered them to Jenny.

"Bella didn't do anything on a small scale. Every kid in town was there."

Jenny raised an eyebrow, prompting him to answer her question.

"I was there too."

"Did Bella really get engaged that night?"

Calvin's expression hardened. He gave a brief nod and began walking toward a room at the end of the foyer. He beckoned Jenny to follow him.

The first thing Jenny spotted when she entered the room was a large, blown up picture of Bella and Calvin arm in arm, hanging on the wall above a bed. It took her a few seconds to realize it had been cut out from a larger group photo, the same one she had seen on Ashley's night stand. Jenny fought a wave of panic and forced herself to appear calm.

"That's us at the junior prom," Calvin said, pointing toward the wall. "I don't know what Bella sees in Jake."

"Was there booze at the party?" Jenny asked.

"Bella ordered a keg," Calvin nodded. "She knew how to keep the kids happy."

"So everyone was drinking and having a good time, huh?"

"Almost everyone," Calvin told her. "I don't drink. I promised my mother I wouldn't touch alcohol until I turned 21."

"What about Bella and Ashley?"

"Bella could drink the best of them under the table. Ashley always tried to imitate her. But she didn't have the stomach for it. I saw her puking her guts out in the bushes."

"What happened after that?"

"They got into Ashley's car," Calvin said. "I saw them myself. Ashley must have had a plan all along."

"You think Ashley crashed her car on purpose, just so Bella would hit her head against the dash? You know Ashley is heavily injured herself?"

Calvin gave a shrug.

"She's d-d-diabolical. She tried to copy Bella all the time but she was never good enough."

"How do you know all this?" Jenny asked. "Did you guys hang out together?"

Jenny thought she knew the answer but she wanted to

hear what Calvin said. She knew Bella and Sam were joined at the hip. They both wore friendship bracelets they had made for each other in junior high. Ashley tagged along with them a lot too. Bella talked about her boyfriend Jake and some other kids from her class but she had never once mentioned Calvin Butler.

"Bella used to be sweet," Calvin said. "Then she fell into some bad company. I had to keep an eye on her."

"Did she ever talk to you?" Jenny asked softly. "Or were you just another kid from her class?"

"W-w-what do you mean?" Calvin stuttered, pushing his glasses up his nose. "Bella was my best friend. She used to hold my hand during recess."

Jenny sensed Calvin was losing his cool. She decided it was best to back off.

"Well, the police must share your opinion of Ashley. They are charging her."

"Finally!" Calvin's eyes gleamed as his mouth settled into a smile. "Bella deserves justice."

"I don't think Ashley wanted to hurt Bella," Jenny said frankly. "But I agree that she was negligent."

"Ashley is just getting what she deserves," Calvin said. "I hope they put her away for a long time."

Jenny said goodbye to Calvin and drove back to the café. She wondered why Calvin was so set against Ashley. Had she been cruel to him in school?

Back at the café, Jenny got busy making lunch. Shrimp po' boys were on the menu and Jenny knew they were Jason's favorite. Jenny got through the lunch rush with her aunt's help and thought of meeting Jason in his office for lunch. He solved her dilemma by calling her over.

Jenny couldn't hide her smile as she liberally sprinkled some Old Bay seasoning on a batch of hot crispy shrimp.

"Get out of here," Star beamed, handing her a basket a few minutes later.

Watery sunlight filtered through clouds and pollen covered the streets like a carpet. Jenny shivered in the salty breeze and hurried across the boardwalk. Jason's office was two doors down from the police station, a place Jenny had visited a lot until a few weeks ago. She walked past the old stone building without a second glance and hurried into Jason's chambers.

"Lunch!" she offered, holding the basket aloft.

"Do I smell shrimp?" Jason asked, rubbing his hands. "You're spoiling me, Jenny."

"It was on the menu," Jenny shrugged. "It's not like I

made it specially for you."

Jason took her hand and spoke softly in her ear.

"But you would have if I had asked you to."

"Only if you had asked me," Jenny teased.

Jason picked up his sandwich and took a hefty bite before narrowing his eyes at Jenny.

"You have something on your mind."

"What will happen to Ashley? Is she going to confess?"

"Not a chance," Jason told her. "She is changing her story."

"What do you mean?" Jenny asked, pouring extra tartar sauce over her po'boy.

"Ashley is saying she was completely sober when she got behind the wheel of that car."

"What?" Jenny exclaimed. "She was singing a completely different tune yesterday. She was blaming herself for Bella's death."

"She might be feeling some remorse," Jason said. "Who wouldn't? But she is changing her official story."

"Is she saying she wasn't drinking at that party? That

won't fly because plenty of people will have seen her."

"She says she was fully alert when she got into that car," Jason elaborated. "This is the kind of technicality lawyers love to make the most of."

"Go on," Jenny prompted Jason.

"Ashley says a deer ran onto the road and she swerved to avoid it. That's when the car hit something else and she lost control."

"Do you believe her?" Jenny asked.

"It could happen to anyone," Jason said. "It all depends on how much alcohol she had consumed."

"She's too young to be a seasoned driver," Jenny said. "She definitely can't be skilled enough to selectively crash that car. She could have died in that accident too. It's a miracle she got away."

"That's what her parents are claiming," Jason nodded. "Her injuries are serious enough to back them up."

"Do you think the police will arrest her now?" Jenny asked.

"I think they are waiting for the autopsy results. My guess is they will move fast after that. I have to be ready to bail Ashley out when the time comes."

"I know you will do everything you can to help that poor girl," Jenny said. "I miss Bella but I can't help feel sorry for Ashley."

Jason placed a call home to talk to Emily. The nanny turned on the speaker phone and they could hear Emily playing with her toys, chattering away in a language only she understood. She recognized Jason's voice right away and clapped her hands. 'Da, Da,' she said.

"Did you hear that, Jenny?" Jason asked, his eyes popping wide.

"I think she's trying to say 'Daddy'," Jenny said, her eyes misting over. "I bet that's going to be her first word."

Jason said goodbye to his daughter and hung up.

"She's the best thing that happened to me, Jenny," Jason sighed happily. "I never knew what I was missing."

Jason was turning fifty that year. He had given up any hopes of being a father. Emily had been a big surprise, one he had embraced with open arms. Jenny thought he was coping really well with the challenges of being an older parent. Hiring a full time nanny had really helped them.

"Why don't you get home early today?" Jenny asked.

"We can have a family dinner. I'll make Emily's favorite meal – peach and carrot puree."

Jason laughed out loud.

"Don't spoil her too much, Jenny."

"I'm not. I'm just teaching her to eat fresh, home cooked food. Nothing wrong with building some healthy habits."

"You're the mom," Jason said. "You know best. I'll try and see you at five."

Jenny felt like she was walking on air on her way back to the café. Jason always made her feel good about herself. She wondered if that was love. Was she falling for her accidental husband?

At the café, Jenny put Jason and Ashley firmly out of her mind and started working on her sundae recipe. She mixed her latest batch of salted caramel in with some vanilla ice cream and toasted walnuts. She poured hot caramel on top of the ice cream and added candied popcorn and crushed pretzels, her special touch. A dollop of whipped cream and a cherry on top sealed the deal.

"That's got my name written on it," Heather said, sweeping into the kitchen.

"Be nice, Heather," Jenny warned. "Didn't your mom

teach you to share?"

The two friends dissolved into giggles as they dug into the frozen treat.

"You nailed this, Jenny," Heather said, giving her a thumbs up. "Go ahead and put this on the menu."

Heather helped her clean up and Jenny drove home an hour later, thinking about Bella.

Chapter 6

It was another sunny spring day in Pelican Cove. Cherry trees were in full bloom and the town looked pretty, festooned with the flowering trees swaying in the breeze under the clear blue skies.

The Magnolias had gathered for their daily cuppa on the deck of the Boardwalk Café. Molly was engrossed in a book while Betty Sue was knitting a yellow scarf. She sneezed rapidly just as Jenny brought out a tray of warm muffins.

"I love spring season, but I hate this pollen," Betty Sue remarked, pulling a tissue out of her bag. "And I hate taking allergy medication. It makes my head go all woozy."

Star laughed while scratching her arms.

"That's the price you pay for living here."

Heather arrived, her eyes glued to her phone as usual.

"Why is everyone so quiet today?" she asked right away. "Something wrong?" She turned toward Jenny. "Is it the baby?"

"The baby's fine," Jenny said with a sigh. "It's just …

it's been a month since we took our trip to the mountains. I can't stop thinking of Bella. She was such a sweet child."

"She got into that car herself," Heather reminded them. "I guess she wasn't really thinking either."

"What have you found out so far, Jenny?" Betty Sue asked. "What really happened?"

Jenny told them about the new information that had surfaced about the accident.

"Ashley insists a deer ran across the road. She reacted instinctively."

"So Bella's death was an accident," Star summed up. "That kid's off his rocker. Is he still claiming Bella was murdered?"

Jenny nodded.

"Calvin seems to think Ashley did it on purpose. But I don't see how she could have without putting her own life in danger. If she did, it was a very stupid move."

"But why would anyone want to harm Bella?" Molly spoke, pulling her head out of her book. "She was an angel."

"I wouldn't go that far," Betty Sue said dourly, clacking her needles. "We hardly knew her."

"Come on, Grandma," Heather protested. "You are hard on everyone. We spent a whole weekend with Bella. We all got to see her first hand. She may have been rich and spoilt, but she had a big heart. Remember that limo she got for us, and that fancy resort she booked?"

"Just showing off," Betty Sue grumbled. "Two days are not enough to know anyone's character."

"So what are you saying, Betty Sue?" Jenny asked. "Bella's gone."

"You can still talk to people who knew her, can't you?" Betty Sue asked. "That's what you do when you want to find out something about a person."

"You're right," Jenny said. "I need to make a list of people who really knew Bella."

"You already talked to Calvin and Ashley," Heather reminded her. "Who else?"

"I'm not sure Calvin exactly knew Bella," Jenny said.

Heather asked her to elaborate but Jenny told her to ignore it for now.

"Aren't you forgetting Sam?" Molly asked. "Bella and Sam were best buds."

"Speaking of …" Heather muttered and tipped her

head toward the beach.

A familiar brown haired figure waved at them. The ladies watched as Sam Hollingsworth ambled across the beach, looking like a giant panda. He came up the steps to the deck and flopped down into a chair, panting from the exertion.

"Hello Sam," Jenny greeted him. "How are you?"

"Missing my favorite girl," he said. "I can't imagine she's gone."

"We were just talking about Bella," Jenny admitted. "She was something else."

Sam looked greedily at the plate of muffins. Jenny offered him one. Sam's face lit up as he picked up two muffins and began eating them at once. He didn't look up until he had devoured both of them.

"Do you have more of these?" he asked Jenny. "I'm starving."

Jenny went in and brought out a fresh batch. Sam grabbed one and made quick work of it.

"Do you know what Calvin Butler is saying?" Jenny asked him.

"That nerd?" Sam asked. "We never gave him time of day."

"So he wasn't friends with Bella?"

"Bella was the queen bee," Sam told them, brushing muffin crumbs off his shirt. "She was a princess, the most popular girl in school. Calvin was invisible. Those two were never going to meet."

Jenny thought of the photo on Calvin's wall but said nothing about it.

"Calvin thinks Bella was murdered," Heather told Sam. "And he thinks Ashley did it."

"Ashley tried to ape Bella all the time," Sam nodded. "Personally, I think she was jealous. But I don't think she had any reason to hate Bella."

"You knew Bella well, didn't you?" Jenny prodded.

"We were besties," Sam bragged. "Bella didn't do anything without talking to me about it. She shared everything with me, you know."

"Did you know she was getting engaged?" Jenny asked.

A look of annoyance flashed across Sam's face for a fraction of a second. Then his face smoothed into a smile.

"Of course I knew. Bella was crazy about Jake."

"What's he like?" Heather asked. "A handsome devil?"

"Jake's a slacker," Sam said flatly. "He wasn't good enough for Bella."

"Does he go to your school?" Jenny asked deliberately.

"Oh no!" Sam said. "Jake dropped out of school long ago."

"How did Bella meet him then?" Jenny wanted to know.

Sam shrugged.

"Somewhere in town, I guess. Maybe at a party? This is a small place. Everyone knows each other."

"How was Bella's family life?" Jenny asked. "Did she get along with her father?"

"Bella's father is a tyrant," Sam told them. "He was always too hard on Bella. He sent her away to school jail."

"What's a school jail?" Heather asked.

"It's one of those places where you send wayward kids. He thought Bella was out of control. All because she liked to go shopping!"

Jenny figured there was more to the story than that. Maybe her father had found out about her alcohol abuse and sent her to some rehab center.

"He thought she was a shopaholic?" Heather asked. "Wasn't she kind of young for that?"

"Bella was so generous," Sam gushed. "She bought me a new wardrobe every season. See these threads?" He pointed to the clothes he was wearing.

Jenny noted they were a pricey brand.

"Bella got these for me," Sam continued. "Her Dad hated that. He's very tight fisted."

"I guess it's his money," Heather pointed out.

"Not really," Sam said with a malicious smile. "Bella came into her trust fund when she turned 18. She had plenty of money at hand. Her Dad ranted and raved but he could do nothing. Bella was free to spend that money anywhere she wanted."

Sam glanced at his watch. It was an expensive smart watch that was all the rage. Jenny recognized it because she had gifted it to her son on his birthday.

"What's for lunch?" Sam asked her. "I'm feeling a bit lightheaded."

"Didn't you just eat four muffins?" Heather burst out.

Sam looked defensive.

"I'm a big guy. I just need to eat more."

"I'm making chicken noodle soup," Jenny told him. "And tuna melts."

Sam brightened and smacked his lips.

"Sounds delicious, Jenny. Don't let me keep you from your work."

The Magnolias dispersed after that. Star had set up her easel on the beach and was painting the seagulls. Heather stayed behind to help Jenny.

Sam followed them into the kitchen. He offered to help and Jenny set him to work stirring the soup.

"Have you been to the hospital to see Ashley?" she asked Sam after a while.

"Ashley is such a wannabe!" Sam said, rolling his eyes. "She's a big mess now."

"Did Ashley and Bella get along?"

"Bella got along with everyone," Sam said, peeping into the refrigerator.

He rearranged some containers and took out a carton of pimento cheese.

"Do you have any crackers to go with this?" he asked.

Jenny pulled a packet of saltines out of a drawer and

shook them out on a plate. Sam settled his ample bulk onto a stool and liberally spread some pimento cheese over the crackers. He put a whole cracker in his mouth at once and began chewing noisily.

"Bella knew Ashley was jealous of her. She was always kind to her though."

"Would Ashley deliberately try to harm Bella?" Jenny asked curiously.

"Nah!" Sam said, scraping the last bit of the pimento cheese from the bottom of the container. "She's too meek. And she loved Bella, even though she envied her."

Jenny chatted with Sam while she grilled the sandwiches, trying to find out more about Bella and her life. Heather stayed busy tapping keys on her phone and taking pictures of the food.

"So you don't think anyone would deliberately want to harm Bella," she asked Sam.

"Her father was the only bad guy in her life," Sam said. "And he was nowhere near her that night. In fact, the whole party was a big secret. Bella was supposed to be studying for a test at Ashley's place."

"Were you drinking at the party too?" Jenny asked.

"I'm 21," Sam said with a shrug. "Almost 22."

Jenny wondered why Sam didn't hang out with kids his age. She decided he was as much of a misfit as Calvin was.

"Why didn't this Jake guy offer to drop Bella home?" Heather asked.

"Jake's too lazy," Sam dismissed. "Ashley always ferried Bella everywhere. They had a pact. Ashley got to use Bella's convertible in exchange for driving her around."

Sam stuck around until Jenny was ready to serve lunch. He ate two bowls of soup and two tuna melts. Jenny packed some cookies for him to take home.

Heather rolled her eyes when he finally left.

"I thought he would never stop eating."

"I guess he has a hearty appetite," Jenny laughed.

"Or he's just plain greedy," Heather quipped.

Jenny was ready to go home a couple of hours later. She decided to visit Ashley at the hospital on the way back. She packed a container of soup for the sick girl. A group of girls in cheerleader uniforms were saying goodbye to Ashley when Jenny got there.

A stack of 'get well soon' cards were propped up on the window sill. The room was full of flowers and balloons. Ashley seemed to have her fair share of friends and well wishers.

"Are you feeling better?" Jenny asked her. "I didn't know you were on the cheerleading team."

"We both were," Ashley told her. "Bella was our captain. We need to elect a new one now. Nationals are coming up next month."

"Will you be well enough to participate?"

Ashley looked sad.

"My cheerleading career is over. I will be lucky if I don't miss my first semester of college."

"Was Bella going to college with you?"

Ashley shook her head.

"She wanted to take a gap year and go to Europe with Jake."

"Did her father know about this?"

"No way! Bella didn't share her plans with Mr. Worthington."

"Are you saying they didn't get along?"

"I'm sure he loved her," Ashley murmured. "But he was pretty strict about everything. Bella had to do everything behind his back."

"You mean he didn't like it when she drank?" Jenny asked with a roll of her eyes.

Jenny knew how tough it was to be a parent to a teenager. When your kids were a certain age, you couldn't do anything right. Her son Nick had given her a hard time when he had been a senior in high school. So when Sam and Ashley badmouthed Bella's father, she took it with a grain of salt.

She needed to go to the horse's mouth. She had to meet Bella's father in person to find out what kind of relationship he had with his daughter.

Chapter 7

Jenny had a dinner date with her husband. The Eastern Shore was home to a lot of fine restaurants. Previously, Jason and Jenny had visited many famed eateries in a one hour radius. That was before Emily came into Jason's life. Jason's busy schedule didn't give him much time to spend with the baby. So they had agreed to have a quiet dinner at home. Jason had offered to fire up the grill so Jenny just had to prepare a few side dishes. She had already marinated the shrimp in Jason's favorite tequila lime marinade. Jason used his own secret spice rub for the steaks.

Emily sat in her high chair at the kitchen counter, banging a spoon on her plate.

"You want more apricot mash?" Jenny asked her. "Your daddy called. He'll be home soon."

Emily's eyes lit up.

"Da, Da, Da," she cried.

Jenny pulled up a stool next to her and started telling her a story. Jason walked in a few minutes later, looking tired but happy.

"How are my girls?" he asked, giving both of them a

hug and a kiss.

"You took long enough," Jenny chided.

"I had quite an eventful day," Jason said, pulling off his tie. "Wait till you hear about it."

"Work can wait," Jenny said. "Let's get dinner first."

They gave full justice to the tasty food. Jenny told Jason to save room for dessert. Emily's eyes were drooping so the nanny took her up to the nursery.

Jenny made a fresh pot of coffee and served Jason's favorite six layer chocolate cake.

"You are spoiling me, Jenny," Jason said with a smile. "I'm going to puff up like a hot air balloon pretty soon."

"You can run an extra mile tomorrow," Jenny told him.

Jason was very particular about going for a run on the beach every morning. Jenny longed to join him but she was busy at the café.

"Emily's doing well now, isn't she?" Jenny asked. "I don't know how she caught that infection. We are not even sending her to daycare yet."

"Relax, Jenny," Jason soothed. "She's a baby. She'll

catch another infection next week. There's only so much we can do to control it."

"She was in such a lot of pain," Jenny said. "It tore my heart, watching her cry."

"You're a softie," Jason smiled, tucking into the cake. "This is amazing, Jenny!"

Jenny took a bite of her own cake and nodded. She had high standards when it came to baking.

"How was your day?" she finally asked Jason. "Any new updates on Bella?"

"Wait till you hear this," Jason nodded. "The autopsy results came back. One of my sources called me this afternoon."

"What does the report say?"

"I don't have access to the whole report," Jason said. "Just part of it. They found poison."

Jenny's mouth dropped open.

"Are you saying someone poisoned Bella?"

Jason nodded his head vigorously.

"It's thrown the police off. They have a whole new line of investigation now."

"We were thinking the impact killed her," Jenny mused.

"Maybe it did," Jason said. "Didn't you take some photos of that car? Did you take a good look at them?"

Jenny banged her fist on the table.

"Silly me. I completely forgot."

She looked around the kitchen for her phone, finally finding it on the coffee table in the living room. Jenny pulled up the photos from the impound.

"The seat belt broke, see?" She pulled up a photo of the torn seatbelt and showed it to Jason. "The impact was so strong the belt snapped in two."

"Go back a bit," Jason said suddenly.

He grabbed the phone from Jenny's hand and flipped back to another photo. He enlarged the part where the belt had snapped.

"This looks like a clean cut," he said. "Do you see what I see, Jenny?"

Jenny peered at the screen and shook her head.

"I think this belt was sawed through with a knife or a pair of shears."

"But why?" Jenny asked, aghast.

"It was done on purpose, of course. The belt was weakened. It might have held the passenger in place otherwise. But the force of the impact made the belt snap."

"I'm a bit confused," Jenny said. "Didn't you say that Bella was poisoned?"

Jason was quiet for a minute.

"It looks like someone made very sure she wouldn't get home alive."

"You are saying the poison and the belt were both the work of the same person?"

"What is the alternative, Jenny?" Jason asked, looking shocked. "One person out for the poor girl's life is bad enough."

"Bella's already gone," Jenny reminded him. "We need to consider every option, however fantastic or horrific it sounds."

"What did Bella do to spawn this kind of hatred?" Jason asked. "You said she was a good person."

"Hatred is not the only motive," Jenny shrugged. "We need to dig deeper."

"What does this mean for Ashley?" Jason wondered out loud.

"Ashley could be guilty if she is the one who tampered with the belt," Jenny told him. "She knew her own seatbelt and airbag would protect her."

"So she drove into a tree at the risk of injuring herself?" Jason's eyebrows shot up questioningly. "She's a high school senior, Jenny. Could she really be that devious?"

"Calvin is convinced Ashley did this. Sam thinks she was jealous of Bella."

"Rivalry is a part and parcel of high school life," Jason quipped. "That doesn't mean kids go around offing each other."

"Ashley is the only one who has come under the radar until now. But what about Bella's family? Her father? I think it's time I paid my respects to him."

"Will you promise to be careful?" Jason urged. "Take Heather with you, please. Don't go alone."

Jason had an appointment in the city the next morning so they turned in early. Jenny's alarm went off at 5 AM and she hurried to the café. She baked a few batches of cranberry orange muffins and made fresh coffee before it was time to open the café.

Her favorite customer greeted her with a smile.

"Are you playing detective again, Jenny?" Captain Charlie asked her. "Is it true that girl was poisoned?"

Jenny was shocked to learn the grapevine had already got hold of Bella's autopsy report.

"I am not sure," she admitted. "But I am going to find out."

Jenny made crab omelets and served the breakfast crowd. Star and Heather both arrived at the same time.

"We are going out," Jenny told Heather, pulling off her apron. She turned to her aunt and winced. "I made chicken salad. I'm going to do my best to get back before lunch."

"Don't worry about a thing," Star told her.

Jenny drove into a cluster of hills that housed Pelican Cove's elite. The Worthingtons lived in a sprawling colonial mansion on a considerable tract of land. Jenny left her car in the portico and burst into the foyer.

"I am here to meet Bella's dad," she told a stern woman clothed in black.

Jenny surmised she was the housekeeper.

"Mr. Worthington doesn't meet anyone without an

appointment."

"This is about Bella," Jenny told her. "Surely he can spare a few minutes to talk about his daughter?"

A tall, blonde man strode up to them. He stared at Jenny with eyes the same blue as Bella's. He had a deep cleft in his chin and his clothes looked like they had been custom made for him.

"Who are you? How do you know my daughter?"

Jenny hadn't expected Max Worthington to recognize her.

"Can we talk?" she asked him.

He looked at his watch and muttered something.

"I can spare ten minutes. I'm a busy man."

Jenny and Heather entered a highly opulent room, decorated in blue and gold.

"I guess you are one of Bella's charity cases?" Max Worthington barked.

"Excuse me?" Jenny shot back.

Max waved a hand around the room.

"As you can see, we are obviously very rich. Bella came into millions when she turned 18. Everyone wanted something from her, you know. They stuck to her like leeches."

"Well, I'm not one of them," Jenny said stoutly. "I am trying to find out who harmed your daughter."

"Why would anyone do that? She was their meal ticket." Max looked at his watch again and cleared his throat. "Are we done here?"

Jenny ignored him and forged ahead.

"How was your relationship with your daughter? Her friends said you were quite heavy handed with her."

"The family had big expectations from Bella. She had high standards to live up to. Unfortunately, she strayed too often."

"My son's in college," Jenny shared. "So I know how hard it is to raise a teenager."

The man's expression softened.

"Bella was a good kid. But she was incapable of understanding the family's stature and their position in society. Our ancestors have worked very hard to build the Worthington name. She was responsible for upholding it.

She grew up without a mother. I tried to discipline her as much as I could but I am a busy man. What can I say? She had plenty of money to indulge herself. She was all set to ruin the family name."

"Did you know she was drinking that night?" Jenny asked. "Did she make a habit of it?"

"I don't know what you are talking about." Max looked away and stared at the massive portrait of the Worthington pioneer hanging over the mantle.

"Word is you sent her to a fancy rehab somewhere for her drug addiction."

Jenny knew she was stretching the truth. She wanted to get some reaction out of Max Worthington. Her efforts were successful.

Max sprang up and glared at her.

"You will not insult my daughter like that."

"That's not my intention," Jenny assured him. "I just want to know more about her."

"My Bella was the sweetest kid you ever met. She was a straight A student. She was captain of the cheerleading squad and also captain of the soccer team. She was going to an Ivy League school up north in the fall."

"Did Bella have a lot of friends?" Jenny asked.

"She was a popular kid. Everyone wanted to be with

Bella."

"What about a boyfriend?"

"You mind what you say about my daughter now," Max growled. "Bella hadn't been presented to society yet. Fraternizing with some boy was out of question. Most of them were charity cases who were after her money anyway. The only boy she talked to was that fat kid who tagged along with her everywhere."

Jenny wondered how Max would react if he heard about Bella's secret engagement.

A tall, blonde girl walked into the room just then. She went and stood beside Max's chair.

"This is my niece, Olivia," Max said. "She just graduated from Brown."

"Who are these people, Uncle?" the girl asked with a smirk. "We need to get going."

Max glanced at his watch again and swore under his breath.

"I'm getting late for my meeting. I assume our business here is done?"

Jenny refused to be rushed.

"You haven't told me how you got along with Bella."

"We had our share of arguments, okay?" Max couldn't hide his frustration. "Bella could be bullheaded. It was partly my fault. I never denied her anything."

"How serious were these arguments?" Jenny pressed.

"What are you implying?" Max demanded. "Bella was my only daughter. She was heir to the Worthington fortune. I was looking forward to the day she would take over the business from me."

Jenny said nothing, prompting him to go on.

"You are seriously mad if you think I had anything to do with my daughter's death."

"You can't believe Bella's death was an accident?" Jenny insisted. "You must have heard about the autopsy report by now. The whole town knows about it."

Max Worthington collapsed into a chair and clutched his forehead with his hands.

"Why would anyone do this to my Bella?"

"I don't know," Jenny said, "but I'm going to find out."

"You stay away from this," Max growled. "I don't want the Worthington name dragged through mud over this. You better not provide more fodder for the tabloids."

Chapter 8

A light drizzle greeted Jenny on her way to the cafe the next morning. Jenny hoped the rain would wash away some of the pollen, bringing some welcome relief from seasonal allergies.

Jenny baked cinnamon rolls for breakfast and made her spiced strawberry glaze to go with them.

The Magnolias arrived earlier than usual, lugging umbrellas and wet jackets. They headed straight to the deck.

"I hope you saved some cinnamon rolls for us," Betty Sue called out as she pulled her knitting out of her bag.

"I made a pan just for us," Jenny told her.

"The spring festival is around the corner," Star reminded her. "Have you decided your menu?"

"I haven't had the time," Jenny clucked. "I was thinking of going with the chicken salad and cupcakes. But I might make some sundaes too."

"It's a great way of trying them out on the crowd," Heather nodded. "We can take plenty of pictures and post them on social media. It will be good advertising,

Jenny."

"Heather told us about the caramel sundae you made," Molly spoke up. "When are we getting to taste it?"

"I'm working on a triple chocolate recipe now," Jenny said. "Why don't you be my taster this time?"

Heather and Molly bickered over what other flavors Jenny could offer. Betty Sue and Star devoted themselves to the cinnamon rolls.

"How was your visit to the Worthingtons?" Betty Sue asked Jenny. "Did Max Worthington give you the time of day?"

"He seemed reluctant at first," Jenny told her.

"The Worthingtons are an old family," Betty Sue said. "They came off the Isabella."

The Isabella was a ship that sank off the coast of Pelican Cove in 1876. There had been a few survivors. Apart from the Pioneers who were the first settlers on the island, the Survivors were some of the oldest inhabitants. They were pretty high up in the island hierarchy.

"Wait," Jenny said. "Does that have anything to do with Bella's name?"

Betty Sue nodded. "The first Worthington on the

island was a mere steward on the Isabella. He got away with a handful of gold before the ship sank. He built a fortune with that money."

"How do you know that, Grandma?" Heather asked. "You have never told me this story."

"My grandpa told me when I was a child," Betty Sue narrated, getting engrossed in her tale. "The first Worthington was a humble man and a hard worker. The Worthingtons were not so high and mighty at that time. Every subsequent generation got richer and started lording it over the rest of us."

"So they owe their fortune to the Isabella?" Jenny asked.

"In a way," Betty Sue nodded. "That's why the oldest daughter in every generation is named after the ship."

"He was strutting around like a peacock, wasn't he Jenny?" Heather remarked, referring to their meeting with Max Worthington.

"He kept harping on family pride and expectations," Jenny agreed. "I guess Bella felt the burden. That's why she acted out."

"Did Bella really do drugs?" Heather asked.

"I don't know, to be honest," Jenny said. "I was just trying to goad him into telling us the truth."

"You could have asked me," Betty Sue grumbled. "He sent that girl to a special boarding school somewhere in the mountains. They were supposed to straighten her out."

"Surely Bella wasn't that bad?" Heather asked. "She was a bit high spirited, I guess. And she squandered money like there was no tomorrow."

"Max didn't care about the money," Betty Sue dismissed. "He wanted her to be prim and proper, like a young lady from a respectable family."

"What is this, the 1950s?" Heather rolled her eyes.

"Bella must have been rebellious," Jenny conceded. "She was drinking at that party, remember? And I'm sure she was dating that boy behind her father's back."

Heather told the Magnolias how Bella hadn't been allowed to have a boyfriend.

"That's archaic!" Star exclaimed.

"Do you think Bella's father found out about Jake?" Molly wondered. "He would be spitting mad if he learnt Bella went and got engaged."

"That's a big motive right there!" Heather pointed out.

"So what?" Star stepped in. "He would rather kill his daughter than have her date someone? That makes no sense to me."

"Worthingtons don't believe in love," Betty Sue said. "Max's marriage was arranged by his father. His wife's family were plantation owners from Richmond."

"Say what you will," Jenny protested. "I can't believe a father will deliberately harm his baby girl."

Betty Sue sighed as she pulled a fresh skein of wool from her bag.

"People like the Worthingtons follow a different moral code. Reputation and family honor means everything to them."

"What about this Jake guy?" Molly asked. "Have any of you met him?"

Jenny shook her head.

"I guess I should go and talk to him some time. I am surprised he hasn't come forward on his own."

"I thought someone said he's a slacker," Heather said. "So what? He's not even bothered about what happened to his fiancée?"

"How serious was this engagement?" Star asked. "Maybe the kids were just having a bit of fun. A reason to party, you know."

"Remember how Bella talked about Jake all the time on our trip?" Jenny reminded them. "She really loved him."

"But did he return those feelings?" Molly questioned. "Or was he just along for a free ride?"

"I still believe Ashley is the top suspect," Heather argued. "She was right there on the spot. And she really clung to Bella like a shadow. It would have been so easy for her to slip something into Bella's drink."

Jenny shook her head.

"Why would she do that? Ashley may have coveted everything Bella had. But I don't think she's capable of any wrongdoing."

"Are you saying that because she's Jason's client?" Heather teased.

"Of course not," Jenny said. "By the way, Heather, what did you think of that girl Olivia?"

"Bella's cousin?" Heather snorted. "She's cut from the same cloth as Max. As snooty as her uncle. Hard to believe Bella came from the same family."

"An old man cornered me when I was backing my car out yesterday," Jenny told the ladies. "He's worked as a gardener for the Worthingtons since Bella was a baby."

"Go on, Jenny," Star prompted. "What did he have to say?"

"He was all torn up about Bella. He told me Olivia was always at loggerheads with her. The two didn't get along at all."

"That doesn't sound like Bella," Star said.

"Olivia is the one who got Bella sent away. She tattled on her all the time. She's always sucking up to Max. The gardener thinks Olivia has an eye on the estate."

"You think Olivia got Bella out of the way so she could be Max's heir?" Heather asked.

"Money is always a strong motive," Molly reminded them. "And there's plenty at stake here, judging by how flush Bella was."

"We don't really know Olivia," Jenny said with a shrug. "She could be rich in her own right."

"Some people can never have enough," Betty Sue pointed out.

"Exactly," Star agreed. "We don't know how greedy this Olivia is. She may not be happy with her share. She wants the whole pie."

"We need to find out more about her," Jenny said. "If Bella and Olivia got into frequent fights, Sam might know about it."

"What about Calvin?" Heather asked Jenny. "Is he still stuck on Ashley as a suspect? What does he have against her anyway?"

"You don't think he's involved in this, do you?" Star wondered. "What if he's accusing Ashley to shift the attention away from himself?"

"Calvin came to me first," Jenny reminded them. "He has always insisted Bella's death was deliberate. Why would he do that if he was guilty?"

"He could be one step ahead of us," Heather said. "He knew what the autopsy results would show."

"Have you met Calvin?" Jenny asked, her hands on her hips. "I don't think he's capable of this kind of deception."

"Say what you will, Jenny," Heather muttered. "I don't trust that kid."

"Looks can be deceptive," Jenny said, defending the nerdy boy. "But I don't mind paying him a visit again."

"Just say when," Heather said. "I'll be the bad cop."

"Yoohooo …" A shrill voice called out from the boardwalk.

The Magnolias gave a collective groan.

A short, plump woman waved at them from the beach and struggled up the café steps.

"How are you, Barb?" Jenny asked kindly.

Barb Norton was a well known figure in Pelican Cove. She spearheaded every initiative and chaired numerous committees. Although she could be a bit pompous, no one could deny that Barb Norton worked hard for the welfare of the town. She had recently been elected mayor.

"I'm doing good, Jenny," Barb panted. "You're just the person I need to talk to."

Barb pulled up an empty chair and collapsed into it. Molly poured her a cup of coffee. Barb looked longingly at the last piece of cinnamon roll resting on a plate. She gave in and tore a piece.

"Delicious," she pronounced. "Are you making these for the spring festival?"

"You think I should?" Jenny asked doubtfully. "I was actually thinking of some kind of sundae with fresh strawberries."

"Sundae?" Barb asked, wagging a finger. "Oh no, Jenny. The Creamery will be selling their ice cream. You don't want to compete with them."

"I'm not ..." Jenny started.

"We don't step on each other's toes here in Pelican Cove," Barb raced ahead. "You should stick to cupcakes or other baked goodies."

Star stepped in to defend her niece.

"Just listen to her, Barb."

"I have already discussed this with the folks at the Creamery," Jenny explained. "I'm going to be using their ice cream for my sundaes. They are fine with it."

"Why didn't you say that before?" Barb grumbled.

"Surely you are not volunteering for the spring festival?" Star asked Barb. "Don't you have official duties as mayor?"

Barb assumed a martyred look.

"The spring festival is my favorite. I am putting in some extra hours to make sure it goes off without a hitch."

"It's high time you stepped aside for some young blood, Barb," Betty Sue boomed. "You are the mayor now. Learn to delegate."

Barb surprised them by agreeing with Betty Sue.

"You are right. I find it hard to relinquish control."

Jenny hid a smile and listened as Barb told them about her plans for the festival. She asked if Heather could help with the online publicity.

Heather squealed with excitement and accepted the responsibility.

"You are entering your child in the Sweet Baby Contest, aren't you?" Barb asked Jenny. "It's her only chance. She will be too old for it next year."

"What will she have to do?" Jenny asked.

"She just has to smile and look pretty," Barb laughed. "Don't worry. She's a shoo-in."

Jenny imagined little Emily wearing the Sweet Baby crown.

"Let me talk to Jason about it, Barb," she promised.

"We have decided to cancel the Island Queen pageant this year," Barb told them. "You know, in memory of that poor girl."

"Did Bella take part in it?" Molly asked.

"Bella Worthington was Miss Island Queen three years in a row. She's going to be sorely missed. We are thinking of renaming the competition after her."

"Aren't there any other pretty girls in town?" Star asked.

"Oh, there are plenty of girls who want that crown," Barb told them. "Some of them are protesting the cancellation."

"Really?" Jenny asked, wondering who was eager to take Bella's place as pageant queen.

Chapter 9

Heather snapped pictures of the strawberry shortcake sundae Jenny had dished up.

"This one is the best so far, Jenny," Heather exhaled. "I can't wait to dig into it."

Cubes of pound cake and white chocolate chips were mixed in with plump, juicy strawberries and vanilla ice cream. Spiced strawberry syrup made the sweet treat even more delectable.

"We are getting late, Heather," Jenny said. "We need to start now if we want to get back before the lunch rush."

"Not before I eat this sundae," Heather told her.

Fifteen minutes later, the girls set off to meet Calvin Butler. Jenny hadn't told him they were coming. She wanted to catch him unawares.

Calvin looked like he had just got out of bed when he opened the door. He was wearing pajamas festooned with planets and asteroids. He ushered them in and poured two glasses of orange juice for them. Then he excused himself and went down a flight of stairs Jenny hadn't noticed before.

"Isn't he a bit old for those PJs?" Heather hissed as she sipped her juice.

Jenny placed a finger on her lips and widened her eyes, warning Heather to be quiet. Calvin returned a few minutes later, dressed in his usual pressed khakis and tightly buttoned up shirt. His hair was slick with some kind of pomade and neatly combed across.

"Do you have any good news?" he asked eagerly. "Please tell me Ashley is going away."

"Why are you so sure Ashley is involved in this?" Jenny asked him.

Calvin licked his lips and pushed his glasses back up his nose.

"Ashley wasn't happy with the engagement, of course. She wanted Jake for herself."

"So now you're saying Ashley was interested in Bella's boyfriend?" Heather scoffed. "That's against the girl code."

"He was her boyfriend first," Calvin said. "Ashley and Jake were a couple all of junior year. They broke up just before the summer."

"Any idea why?" Jenny asked.

Calvin shrugged.

"Ashley is ambitious. Jake's too easygoing for her."

"If Ashley dumped him before, why would she be interested in him now?" Heather asked.

"Don't you see?" Calvin said, sounding frustrated. "Ashley wanted everything Bella had. When Bella fell in love with Jake, Ashley wanted him back."

"So Ashley got Bella out of the way?" Jenny considered. "That sounds cold blooded."

"That's the kind of person she is," Calvin smirked.

"How good are you with these new fangled phones?" Jenny asked suddenly.

"What does that have to do with Bella?" Calvin asked, puzzled.

"Nothing. Heather's been having some issues. Can you help her out?"

"My Mom's the same," Calvin said. "She has a hard time using all the settings on her phone."

Heather played along and asked Calvin how she could lock her phone with a code. Jenny asked Calvin where the bathroom was.

"Down the hall to your right," Calvin said, engrossed in tapping some keys on Heather's phone.

Jenny walked in the direction Calvin had pointed to. Then she backtracked a bit and rushed down the flight of stairs Calvin had used earlier. As she had surmised, she entered a fully furnished basement.

A black leather couch was placed in front of a big TV. A treadmill and some exercise equipment occupied one corner of the room. A large bed was visible behind a decorative screen. Jenny walked closer to the bed and glanced at the wall next to it. Her mouth dropped open in surprise.

She hurried up the stairs, hoping Calvin hadn't noticed how long she had been gone.

"There you go," Calvin was telling Heather. "It's very easy, really. But you need to remember your code, okay?"

Heather thanked him profusely and looked at Jenny.

"Tell us more about the party, Calvin," Jenny said. "Do you know when the girls left?"

"I was keeping an eye on Bella," Calvin nodded.

Calvin's words took on a new significance in light of what Jenny had seen in the basement.

"That was very kind of you," she said. "Was Bella sober when they left?"

Calvin grew anxious. He shook his head vigorously.

"They were both very drunk. I offered to drive them home, you know. If only Bella had listened to me."

"You have a car?" Jenny asked.

"I borrowed my Dad's car for the party," Calvin told them. "I followed the girls to keep an eye on them. It happened right before my eyes."

"Did you see the deer?" Jenny asked.

"What deer? Ashley seemed to yank her wheel suddenly and crashed into the tree. It was an awful sight."

Calvin stuck to his story. He promised to call Jenny if he remembered anything else. Jenny and Heather said goodbye and started back.

"You know what we are missing?" Jenny asked. "Jake."

"We need to hunt this guy down," Heather agreed. "Maybe Sam will know where we can find him."

"I have a better idea," Jenny said. "Let's go back to the café now."

Jenny dropped Heather off at the Bayview Inn before going back to the café. She sliced red, green and yellow peppers for making quesadillas. Star handled the cash register while she took charge of the grill in the kitchen. Lunch progressed slowly, mainly because Jenny was impatiently waiting for her favorite customer.

She hurried out when she heard the familiar voice.

"Lunch is on the house today," she told Captain Charlie. "It's something different from your usual sandwich."

"I'll eat anything you cook, Jenny," the old salt said with a grin. "What's going on in that razor sharp mind of yours?"

"You know that boy Jake?" Jenny asked. "Any idea where I can find him?"

"You're in luck," Captain Charlie told her. "I saw him on the beach out back earlier. Tall and blonde with a red cooler by his side."

"Thanks, Captain Charlie. Your lunch is coming right up."

Jenny rushed out to the deck and scanned the beach, shading her eyes with her hand. She spotted the red cooler right away. A handsome young boy sat on a camp chair, sipping a can of soda, staring out to the sea.

Jenny walked over to him.

"Are you Jake?" she asked.

The boy scratched a spot above his ear and looked up. Jenny could barely see his eyes through the dark shades.

"You're the lady from the café," he said. "Bella told me all about you."

"I am sorry for your loss," Jenny offered. "You must miss her."

The boy's eyes flickered a bit.

"Bella was so happy that night," Jake said. "She wanted us to elope. She said her father couldn't do much once we got married. He would have to come around."

"Have you ever met him?" Jenny asked, noticing a big stain on the shirt Jake was wearing.

His clothes looked crumpled and dirty, like they hadn't been washed for a while.

"The mighty Max Worthington?" Jake drawled. "Nah!"

"Someone said you dropped out of school."

"Why bother?" Jake shrugged. "I can't afford college anyway. I go out on the crab boats. It's enough to get by."

"Bella had plenty of money for the two of you, didn't she?"

"You think that's what I wanted from her?" Jake asked.

He didn't seem to be offended by Jenny's insinuation.

"Do you know Calvin Butler? He is saying Ashley killed Bella."

"That nerd?" Jake dismissed. "I wouldn't believe a word he says."

"You know Bella was poisoned, don't you?" Jenny asked. "That does suggest someone was up to no good."

"The police are looking into it, aren't they?"

"Aren't you even a little bit curious?"

Jake swallowed the last of his soda and gave a loud burp.

"It won't bring her back."

"Did you even love her, Jake?" Jenny asked, irritated by Jake's indifferent responses.

Jake picked up his cooler and walked away without a word, leaving Jenny staring at his back. Jenny wasn't sure if Jake was being callous or if he was just a private person.

"That was a bust," she muttered to herself as she went inside the café.

Star was waiting for her with a platter of quesadillas.

"The café's almost empty," she told Jenny. "Time to eat, sweetie."

Jenny was so wrapped up in her thoughts, it took her a while to notice Star was just picking at her food.

"Are you feeling well?" she asked, concerned. "Tri pepper quesadillas are your favorite."

"I'm fine," Star said, pushing her plate aside. "It's just …"

Jenny topped up her aunt's sweet tea and urged her to go on.

"What do you think about Jimmy?"

"Your Jimmy? Jimmy Parsons?" Jenny asked. "He's a good man. You guys are getting along well, aren't you?"

"A bit too well," Star said under her breath.

"What does that mean?" Jenny wanted to know.

Her aunt had been a lonely widow for several years.
Jimmy Parsons had dated her briefly when she first
came to Pelican Cove. Then Star fell in love with her
husband and married him. Jimmy fell into bad habits
and earned the reputation of being the town drunk.
But Jimmy had always had a soft spot for Star. They
had rekindled their friendship in the past couple of
years. With Star's help and encouragement, Jimmy had
kicked his habit and had been sober for over a year.
They were taking things slowly, happy spending time
with each other.

"Jimmy wants us to be a couple."

Jenny tried to hide a smile.

"Aren't you already a couple, Star?"

"Who said that?" Star asked, looking cornered. "Did
someone say that, Jenny?" She took a big gulp of her
tea and her mouth set in a firm line. "We are just
friends."

"So are you moving in together?" Jenny asked.

"What?" Star exclaimed. "No! I am not even ready to
be a couple."

"Why are you so hung up on labels?" Jenny asked
kindly. "You do like him, don't you?"

Star's cheeks turned pink. Jenny was surprised to see

her aunt blushing.

"He makes me laugh," Star admitted. "And he's thoughtful and caring. He's just nice, Jenny."

"Well then …"

"I suppose we are good friends," Star said haltingly.

"Or more than friends?" Jenny quirked an eyebrow. "I have seen how he looks at you."

"Pish posh," Star said, her face turning red as a tomato.

"Do you love him back?" Jenny pushed.

Star gave a tiny shrug.

"What are you afraid of?" Jenny asked her. "You don't think he'll fall off the wagon again?"

"I don't care about that," Star said earnestly. "I know Jimmy is taking it one day at a time. He has my full support. Things have been hard for him. Even if he does make a mistake, I will make sure he gets back on track again."

"What are you afraid of then?" Jenny asked, puzzled.

"You know how people talk in this town," Star said. "What will people say?"

"That you are taking a second chance at love?"

"I'm pushing seventy, Jenny. I'm too old for this."

"You don't mean that," Jenny said, draining her glass of sweet tea. "Like you said, you are in the twilight of your life. You should do what makes you happy. If that means giving a name to your relationship, so be it."

"Jimmy won't stop at this," Star said. "What if he wants to move in together, or worse, get engaged? I am not ready for that."

"Take it one thing at a time, and enjoy the ride."

Star plunged into thought at Jenny's short but sweet advice.

"And let me tell you one thing," Jenny told Star with a smile. "The town already knows about you and Jimmy!"

Chapter 10

Jenny sat out on her patio, sipping a glass of wine, admiring the roses blooming in her garden. She had just finished putting dinner together and was waiting for Jason to come home. The spring evening was pleasantly warm, and Jenny enjoyed the light breeze coming off the ocean.

Jason arrived soon after and called out to Jenny.

"Over here," Jenny replied, pouring some wine for Jason.

Jason came out on the patio, holding a large gaily wrapped package.

"Surprise!" he said, looking as eager as a little boy. "I hope you like it, Jenny."

Jenny took the package from him and tore it open. It was a picture of them on their wedding day. Due to the abrupt nature of their wedding, they hadn't taken the usual wedding photos. Heather had forced them to pose and clicked a few pictures with her phone.

"This was the best one Heather had," Jason told Jenny.

"I'm going to hang this in our room," Jenny promised.

"Or do you prefer the living room?"

"You can put it anywhere you want, Jenny," Jason said, giving her a quick hug. "Can you believe we are really married?"

Jenny wondered how real her marriage was. Jason did so many little things to spoil her. But he had always liked to spoil Jenny. Jenny realized she hadn't given Jason a wedding gift or done anything special for him.

"You don't need to get me anything," Jason said, reading her mind. "Having you here with me, in this moment, is all I want in life."

"Does that mean you don't want any dinner?" Jenny teased.

Jason placed a hand on his flat stomach.

"I'm starving, Jenny. Something smells good."

"I made pasta primavera. We had fresh asparagus from Heather's garden. Let's go eat."

Jason went up to look in on the baby.

"She had a play date today," Jenny told him when he came down. "She's exhausted."

Jenny had made caprese salad, Jason's favorite. Jason took a second helping of the pasta and looked longingly at the tiramisu Jenny placed before him.

"Can we have this a little later?" he asked. "I'm so full I can barely eat another bite."

Jenny put their plates in the refrigerator and sat down.

"Any new developments regarding Bella?" she asked.

"Things are moving slowly," Jason said. "The police are being very tight lipped."

"We should find out more about this poison," Jenny spoke. "Isn't poison supposed to be a woman's weapon of choice?"

"That's what they say," Jason agreed. "It doesn't help Ashley's case. She's the only woman we know connected with Bella."

Jenny thought about Bella's cousin Olivia. She told Jason about her.

"You are saying this girl inherits the Worthington fortune now that Bella's gone?"

"Sure looks like it," Jenny nodded. "That gives her a very strong motive."

"Why does she need money? Isn't she a trust fund kid too, like Bella?"

"I'm not sure about that," Jenny said. "But I can find out."

"Cousins quarrel all the time," Jason considered. "That doesn't mean she would actually hurt Bella. They were family."

Jenny decided she had to find out more about Olivia and Bella's relationship. She needed to talk to Sam. She fired off a text message from her phone, inviting Sam to come to breakfast at the Boardwalk Café. Perpetually hungry, she knew Sam would never turn down a free meal.

The next morning, Jenny woke up when her alarm went off and rushed through her shower. She watched the sun rise over the ocean as she sipped her first cup of coffee, standing out on the deck of the café. The early morning air had a nip to it but the clear skies foretold another sunny day.

Jenny got to work making spinach and bacon omelets loaded with three types of cheese. She had blueberry muffins and strawberry parfaits on hand, plenty to satisfy even Sam.

Being Friday, a fresh wave of tourists had descended on Pelican Cove. Jenny barely had time to look up when Sam ambled in around 8 AM. She offered him a table on the deck out back and promised to look in on him.

Sam kept himself entertained sampling every item on the menu. Jenny got some respite when Star arrived, and she went out to talk to Sam.

"How are you holding up without Bella?" she asked.

"She left a big void. I don't know what to do with myself half the time."

"Tell me about Olivia," Jenny prompted.

"She was mean!" Sam said, cutting a piece of his omelet with excessive force. "Made my Bella cry more than once."

"Wasn't she away at college?"

"She came here during breaks," Sam explained. "Olivia was a favorite with Bella's father. He wanted Bella to be like her."

"I thought Bella was a straight A student," Jenny mused. "Plus she was ahead in all kinds of extracurricular activities. Her father should have been proud of her."

"Bella's social life bothered him. He was afraid she would sully the Worthington name. He's pretty crazy when it comes to the family's reputation."

"What does Olivia have to do with all this, Sam?"

"Olivia talked down to Bella all the time. She was a big bully. And she went running to Mr. Worthington every time Bella sneezed. She managed to make a simple shopping trip sound scandalous."

"What did she want?"

"It's clear, isn't it?" Sam asked, picking up a parfait cup. "Olivia wanted to be the favorite. And she was, if you ask me."

"But she's not Bella's sister, is she?" Jenny argued. "She's just a cousin."

"She's the only Worthington heir now that Bella is gone," Sam pointed out. "It helps that Max already thinks highly of her."

"She's barely older than Bella. You think she would actually do anything to harm Bella?"

"All I know for sure is Bella's not with us anymore," Sam said, pushing his plate away. "And Olivia did everything she could to make her life miserable."

"You think Olivia could have told Max Worthington about Jake?"

"She wouldn't keep it to herself. You can bet on it."

Sam left to go to school. Jenny tried to evaluate if Olivia was just a bully or worse. The Magnolias arrived at their usual time. Jenny didn't say much as she brought out the coffee and muffins.

"Something on your mind?" Heather asked her.

"Olivia and Bella were almost like sisters."

"You don't want her to be guilty, do you?" Heather asked. "You need to be objective here, Jenny."

Jenny pondered over Heather's words as she made chicken salad for lunch. She couldn't accept that Bella had been close to whoever was responsible for her death.

An old man wearing a suit and a driver's cap came up to the counter. He ordered lunch and asked Jenny if he could talk to her. Jenny ushered him to a table.

"I work for Mr. Worthington," the man started. "I was Miss Bella's driver."

Jenny gave the man a once over. He was tall and muscular and Jenny placed his age at around fifty. She figured he had doubled as a bodyguard for the rich girl.

"I thought Ashley drove Bella everywhere."

The man looked uncomfortable.

"It was supposed to be our secret. Miss Bella was embarrassed she didn't have a license. She was mighty scared of getting behind the wheel."

Jenny had an inkling of how a teen girl's mind might work.

"She thought the other kids would laugh at her, I guess."

The driver nodded.

"Miss Bella was popular but she could be insecure. That cousin of hers talked her down all the time."

"So Olivia knew Bella didn't drive?" Jenny asked sharply. "What about her father?"

"Mr. Worthington doesn't know," the driver said. "He would be spitting mad if he did. He wanted Miss Bella to be perfect in everything."

"How did Olivia find out?"

"She was always sneaking up on Miss Bella. Then she would snitch on her. She's a mean one."

"What did you do when Ashley drove Bella around?" Jenny asked.

"I drove Ashley's car," the driver explained. "I used to be right behind them. They didn't like it but it was the only way I would let Ashley drive the Mercedes. I was supposed to keep an eye on Miss Bella. I couldn't let her out of my sight."

"Where were you on the night of the accident?" Jenny asked.

The driver hung his head.

"Miss Bella insisted I take the night off. I had no idea the girls would be drinking. I should have stayed on and seen Miss Bella home safely."

"There's no point in blaming yourself now," Jenny consoled him. "I guess they just didn't want any grownups around."

"If only I hadn't listened to Miss Bella ..." The driver's eyes turned misty. "I could never say no to her. I have been ferrying her around since she was knee-high."

"You must have known her well. Did she have any enemies? Anyone who was out to get her?"

The man shook his head.

"Everyone loved Miss Bella. She didn't let her money get to her head. She was kind to people. She didn't think twice about helping a friend out, or donating money to those who needed it."

"Do you know she was poisoned?" Jenny asked.

"I heard about that," the driver said. "I can't imagine

someone doing it on purpose."

"What about Ashley's car?" Jenny asked. "Was it even roadworthy?"

"That's what I wanted to talk to you about," the driver said. "I drove Ashley's car all the time. It was old but it was in good condition. I made sure of that."

"So there was nothing wrong with the car then," Jenny sighed.

The driver looked over his shoulder and leaned toward Jenny.

"I managed to take a look at it. Buddy of mine knows the bloke who works at the impound."

Jenny folded her hands, waiting eagerly for him to go on.

"I took a good look at that seatbelt and I can tell you it didn't snap on its own. Someone cut it with a knife."

Jenny rapped the table with her hand.

"That's what I thought."

"That's not all," the man continued. "I was keeping an eye on the car that night. This was before Miss Bella told me to go home. I saw a kid get into the car."

"What did this kid do exactly?" Jenny asked.

"Couldn't tell for sure," the driver said. "He was already in the car when I noticed him. I yelled and hurried toward the car. But he ran out before I could get there."

"Any idea who it was?" Jenny asked.

"It wasn't one of Miss Bella's friends," the driver said. "But I will never forget him - some kid with thick glasses and a face full of acne."

"I think I know who that is," Jenny muttered, thinking of Calvin Butler.

The driver took a sip of his tea and looked at Jenny beseechingly.

"Word around town is that you are trying to find out what happened to Miss Bella. I am ready to help any way I can."

"You have already been a big help," Jenny assured him. "Thank you for sharing this with me. I won't rest until I find out what happened to Bella."

The driver seemed comforted as he finally took a bite of his sandwich.

Jenny remembered the fancy Swiss knife Calvin had pulled out of his pocket when she was visiting him.

Had Calvin Butler sawed through the seatbelt in
Ashley's car?

Chapter 11

Jenny tossed and turned in bed, thinking about what Bella's driver had told her. Emily started crying in the middle of the night. Jenny sat with her, trying to entertain her in different ways. But Emily wouldn't stop being fussy. Jenny crooned a lullaby her grandmother used to sing to her. Star appeared outside the baby's room.

"Do you think she might be hot?" she asked Jenny. "The heat's on in the house but it's not that cold outside."

Jenny cracked a window open, letting some fresh air in. Emily settled down after a few minutes, finally closing her eyes.

"Time to switch the heat off, I guess," Star said with a yawn. "It's the changing seasons. The weather's completely out of whack. The baby feels it too, I guess."

Jenny's head barely hit her pillow when the alarm went off. Jenny couldn't stop yawning as she got ready for her day. She decided she needed something to uplift her mood and chose a tie dyed top Star had got for her.

A light drizzle greeted Jenny on her way to work. Pelican Cove was in for an overcast day.

At the Boardwalk Café, Jenny slid the muffins in the oven and started cutting avocadoes. Her avocado and egg toast had become very popular with tourists and locals. She set some aside for Molly and Heather who loved them. The older Magnolias didn't care for the hip creation. Betty Sue called it a fad.

Jenny worked through the breakfast rush and baked a fresh batch of blueberry muffins for the Magnolias. Betty Sue arrived, knitting something in blue wool as she walked.

"It's a pair of booties for Emily," she told Jenny. "I'm making her a pair in all the Easter colors."

"You spoil her too much, Betty Sue," Jenny said with a smile.

"She's the only baby around here," Betty Sue huffed. "I have been waiting for a young one in the family for years."

Heather ignored the suggestive look her grandma directed at her.

The ladies went out on the deck and settled down at their favorite table. A bank of clouds skirted the horizon, making the atmosphere muggy.

"Any updates on Bella?" Betty Sue asked, taking a sip of her coffee.

Jenny told them about her meeting with Bella's driver.

"Are you sure this boy Calvin cut the seatbelt?" Molly asked. "I've never met him but I find it hard to believe he would do anything like that. Based on your description, he seems socially awkward. But that doesn't mean he would deliberately harm anyone."

"There's another reason I think he wouldn't harm Bella," Jenny sighed.

She told them about what she had seen in Calvin's basement.

"What kind of pictures, Jenny?" Heather asked. "Kids like pinning up photos of their friends."

"There were dozens of them," Jenny said, "a whole wall full. All of them were of Bella. Some of them were even a bit voyeuristic, like some pictures of her swimming in a pool, or sun bathing on the beach."

"What are you saying?" Molly asked, horrified. "You think he followed her around and took those photos without her knowledge?"

Jenny nodded her head vigorously.

"The driver didn't recognize Calvin. That means Bella

didn't really hang out with him."

"But that's not the impression he gave us," Star spoke up. "Since the first time he came to you, he always projected he was a great friend of Bella's."

"I thought so too," Jenny admitted. "But I guess I was mistaken."

"So you're saying he is some kind of weirdo?" Heather asked.

"It does look like he was stalking Bella," Jenny mused.

"So Bella had a psycho stalker!" Heather exclaimed loudly. "And no one knew about him?"

"Bella was always in the limelight, wasn't she?" Molly asked. "If some kid was following her around all the time, surely someone must have spotted him."

"Calvin is a nerd," Jenny told her. "The type of kid that's almost invisible in high school."

"Teenagers can be cruel," Molly agreed. "Why do you think this kid was obsessed with Bella though? I can't imagine her being cruel with him."

"No," Jenny agreed. "Bella wasn't like that. I think she was just completely unaware of his presence."

"And Calvin was secretly in love with her," Heather

said, shaking her head.

"Bella's engagement must have cut him up," Molly pointed out. "You think it made him flip?"

"It does give him a motive," Jenny said thoughtfully.

"It gives him a very strong motive," Heather stressed. "Just think about it. He's been mooning over this girl forever, thinking she might throw him a scrap or two. Then she goes and declares her love for someone else. I bet he was plenty mad."

"That could have prompted him to cut the seatbelt," Jenny said. "But I can't believe he would want to harm Bella."

"Love, especially unrequited love, can turn to hatred in an instant," Molly told them. "You never know what's going on in someone's mind."

"You're saying this boy is crazy?" Star asked.

"He's always seemed a bit off to me," Heather chimed in.

Jenny seemed to make up her mind.

"What's the point of all this speculation? I think it's time to go straight to the source."

"Be careful, Jenny," Molly warned. "He might get

violent if you openly confront him."

Heather and Star exchanged a look. Jenny noticed Star give a barely perceptible nod.

"What are you two plotting?" Jenny asked her aunt.

Star cleared her throat.

"Why don't you let the police handle this, Jenny?"

Jenny's face hardened.

"We don't know what Calvin is up to exactly. It might be too premature to involve the police."

"On the contrary," Heather plunged in. "I think that kid is unreliable. You will be better off collaborating with the police on this one."

"I'm just going to talk to him," Jenny protested.

"Take Adam with you," Heather said in a rush. "He'll be on hand if something goes wrong."

"Are you out of your mind, Heather?" Jenny asked. "I haven't talked to Adam since the day of the wedding."

"The day he so cruelly dumped her at the altar," Molly said, taking Jenny's side. "Jenny would rather drop this whole case than go talk to that numbskull."

Heather chewed on her bottom lip and stared at Jenny.

"He was asking about you. He's worried you are putting yourself in danger again."

"Are you meeting Adam behind my back?" Jenny asked Heather coldly. "What exactly are you telling him, Heather?"

Heather looked flustered. "You know me better than that, Jenny. Please don't misunderstand."

"You have managed to shock me, Heather," Jenny said, gripping her chair tightly. "I don't know what I am supposed to think."

"I ran into Adam yesterday at the seafood market," Heather told her. "It's the first time I met him since … he's lost a lot of weight. He looked awful, Jenny."

Jenny swallowed a lump and stared out at the sea.

"I'm not interested in learning anything about Adam."

"He wanted to know what you thought about Bella's death. I told him you were looking into it."

Jenny gave Heather a quelling look.

"Adam wants you to watch your back," Heather rushed forward. "He offered to help any way he can."

"Too little too late," Betty Sue snorted. "Those Hopkins boys were always trouble."

"You stay away from him, Jenny," Star spoke up. "You have just started bonding with Jason."

Jenny held up a hand.

"Thanks for all the advice but I know what I am going to do. And we will not talk about Adam again."

Jenny stomped off the deck, leaving the Magnolias staring at her back.

"Are you an imbecile?" Betty Sue thundered at Heather. "Look what you did."

"I think that went well," Heather said, making a face. "Jenny needs to be realistic. She's bound to run into Adam somewhere or the other."

"It's too soon, Heather," Molly said. "Give her some time."

"I fully support Jenny on this one," Star said stoutly. "Adam Hopkins is dead to me."

The Magnolias squabbled over how Jenny should deal with Adam. It was rare for them to argue over anything. They were so engrossed in their bickering, none of them spotted Jason hurrying along the boardwalk toward the café. He bounded up the steps and rapped on the table to get their attention.

"Jason!" Molly exclaimed. "Did Jenny call you over?"

Jason's brows were bunched together in a frown. It was such a rare expression for him, the Magnolias forgot about their fight and stared at him in alarm.

"Where is she?" he asked. "Where's my Jenny?"

"She'll be fine, Jason," Star said in a steady voice. "Don't get your knickers in a twist."

Jason looked at her uncomprehendingly.

"Didn't Jenny call you here?" Star asked.

Jason shook his head. "There's been a development."

Jenny came out on the deck just then.

"Have they arrested Ashley?"

Jason rushed to his wife and held both her hands in his.

"It's Calvin Butler. I'm sorry, Jenny. He's dead."

Jenny's mouth dropped open in shock.

"When did that happen? I was planning to go see him today."

"They found him this morning," Jason told her, ushering her to a chair. "Poor kid hung himself."

Everyone started talking at once. Molly felt sorry for

Calvin. Heather looked like the cat that had swallowed the canary.

"What did I tell you, Jenny? He was guilty all along."

"Let's not jump to conclusions," Jenny cautioned.

"How much more proof do you need?" Heather argued. "He must have realized you were on to him."

"How would he know that?" Jenny asked. "That doesn't make sense."

"Do you think Bella's driver went and saw Calvin?" Molly asked.

"We don't know how many people this driver talked to," Star said. "He might have said something to Bella's father."

"That's not likely," Jenny dismissed. "Bella and the driver had an understanding. Max Worthington knew nothing about it."

"Did he leave a suicide note?" Betty Sue asked Jason.

"The police are being tight lipped," Jason informed them. "There's very little information available at this time."

"So we are not sure what exactly happened to Calvin?" Jenny asked. "Poor boy."

"He was convinced someone was out to get Bella," Molly said. "And now he's no more."

"Molly has a point, Jenny," Jason said. "I think you should stop sleuthing around now."

"What?" Jenny exclaimed. "I need to find out what happened to Bella, Jason."

"Let the police handle it," Jason said firmly. "Things are heating up, Jenny. You need to think about your own safety."

"I'm fine," Jenny said, rolling her eyes. "I can take care of myself."

"You are not alone now, Jenny," Betty Sue chimed in. "What about the baby?"

"Jenny will never do anything to endanger Emily," Jason said. "I trust her completely."

"But she's a married woman now," Betty Sue argued. "Shouldn't her family come first?"

"There is no competition here, Betty Sue," Jason said, wagging a finger at her. He turned toward Jenny. "I admire your independence, Jenny. It's what I fell in love with. But let's not forget there's a killer out there. We have no idea who it is or what he is capable of."

"I promise I will be careful," Jenny pleaded.

"Calvin is no more," Heather pointed out. "You don't have a client now, Jenny."

"I don't need one," Jenny told them. "I am doing this for Bella."

"We underestimated Calvin's grief," Molly said. "He missed Bella so much he took his own life."

"Or," Heather said, pausing dramatically. "He couldn't handle the guilt."

Chapter 12

The town hall was packed with standing room only. Betty Sue sat on one end of a makeshift stage with a couple other bigwigs from town. Max Worthington sat at the other end, glancing at his watch every few seconds. Barb Norton stood at the podium, trying to get the crowd to settle down.

Jenny sat between Heather and Molly in the first row. Jason and Star were in a row behind them.

"This is a waste of time," she grumbled. "I would rather work on my sundae recipe."

"Hush," Heather said, poking her with an elbow. "Barb has some announcement. This is going to be good."

"Probably something controversial," Molly laughed.

"More like idiotic," Star said from behind them. "As if she doesn't have enough on her plate already."

"Wonder what Max Worthington is doing here," Jenny mused. "I have never seen him at these meetings before."

"He's too high and mighty for town hall meetings,"

Star supplied. "The Worthingtons think they are better than the Newburys. I say they are both crooks."

The Newburys were one of the wealthiest families in town, rumored to have built their fortune from sunken treasure.

"I guess they both got rich off the Isabella," Jenny spoke out loud, referring to the ship that had sunk in the shoals around the island.

"But the Worthingtons look down on the Newburys," Star told her.

"I can't keep track of this island politics," Jenny muttered. "I think it's silly."

The crowd went quiet just then and Jenny's words rang out in the silence. Every pair of eyes in the room turned toward her.

Barb Norton banged her gavel before the crowd could erupt again.

"Welcome to this special meeting," Barb spoke loudly into the microphone. "I am sure you are all excited about the spring festival."

A few snide remarks were made, eliciting a few laughs from the audience. Barb glared at the crowd, making eye contact with the people who had dared to laugh at her.

"I have an action plan for making the spring festival bigger and better," Barb intoned. "But we have another item on the agenda before we talk about that."

Max Worthington stood up and came forward.

Barb continued. "As some of you may know, the Worthington family lost their daughter recently in a tragic accident."

A hush fell over the audience.

"Her father, Max Worthington, is here to announce a scholarship in her name."

Max Worthington cleared his throat. He kept his words brief. The Worthington family would sponsor one student's entire college education each year. A board of trustees would decide who the scholarship would be awarded to. Eligibility criteria would be disclosed later.

Max didn't wait for the applause to die down. He stepped off the stage and walked out of the room with a heavy gait, looking like a man carrying a big burden. Jenny felt sorry for him.

Barb was banging her gavel again.

"I am proposing Pelican Cove's first film festival," she said. "It can run along with the spring festival or the week before it. This will help us attract more tourists to the town, giving a big boost to business."

"We don't need more tourists," a voice piped up from the back.

Peter Wilson, the local auto shop owner was standing up, shaking his head vigorously.

"I warned you about this," he spoke, pointing a finger at the crowd. "More tourists increase the burden on our town. We don't want to be another Venice, do we?"

"What's he blathering about?" One old woman asked the man sitting next to her.

"Now, Peter," Barb said in a warning tone. "You had your chance. You lost the election, remember? I am free to push my agenda as mayor."

"You are making a big mistake," Peter Wilson snapped. "Mind my words, Barb."

Someone pulled Peter down in his seat.

"What kind of movies are you going to show at this festival?" Betty Sue asked Barb. "They better be something everyone can watch."

"That depends on the theme," Barb Norton replied. "But we will try to choose movies suitable for general viewing."

"Where are you going to play these movies?" someone asked from the crowd. "Is it going to be like a drive-in?"

"It's not warm enough for that yet," someone objected.

"It's plenty warm," another voice butted in.

"We were thinking of holding the festival right here," Barb told them.

"This place is too small, Barb." Star gave her opinion. "Especially if you are expecting the locals and the tourists to show up for it."

"Are you going to charge admission?" a voice from the crowd asked.

"Locals shouldn't be charged anything," a woman with a toddler in her arms called out. "Make the tourists pay!"

"I agree," Betty Sue thundered from her perch. "Make a note of that, Barb."

Barb was beginning to look frazzled.

"We are accepting all ideas regarding the film festival for the next two days. There will be a box outside my office. We will make a final decision based on that and talk about it at the next town meeting."

"That was a drag," Jenny griped as everyone began filing out.

Jason put an arm around her and hugged her close.

"Are you feeling unwell? You love these meetings."

"I guess I'm distracted," Jenny sighed.

"How's Nick?" Jason asked, inquiring after Jenny's son. "It's been a while since he came for a visit."

Nick went to college in the city and was a very busy young man.

"He's going to try and come home this weekend," Jenny told Jason, sounding hopeful.

Heather wove her arm around Jenny's and pulled her apart from Jason.

"Don't forget we are coming over," she reminded her. "Your husband won't mind, will he?"

Jason took a playful jab at Heather.

"Her husband doesn't mind as long as he's invited."

"Tradition demands that this be a girls only night," Heather said. "But some things will have to change now that Jenny is married, I guess."

"You betcha," Jason nodded.

They made tracks toward Mama Rosa's, the best pizzeria in town. It was also the only local pizza shop and most people from the town hall meeting had made a bee line for it.

The girls huddled in a corner, chatting with the town people while Jason went in. He came back lugging several large boxes.

Fifteen minutes later, they were all sitting in front of a blazing fire in Jenny's living room. Jenny stole upstairs to look in on the baby. Emily was sleeping peacefully in her little bed, sucking on her thumb.

Jason was just getting off a phone call when Jenny came downstairs.

"Bad news?" she asked, steering him into the kitchen with a nod.

"You are not going to like this, Jenny," Jason said, running his hand through his hair. "That was one of my sources at the police station. It looks like Calvin couldn't have hung himself."

Jenny stared at Jason, wide eyed.

"That poor kid! Are you saying he didn't take his own life?"

Jason nodded.

"Something about the height of the stool," he murmured. "The police have opened an investigation."

"Ashley's still in the hospital, isn't she?" Jenny asked. "She couldn't have done this."

"Actually, they discharged Ashley a couple of days ago. She's home but she has a nurse looking after her round the clock. And she can barely stand up."

"Calvin may have been a stalker, but I don't think he wanted to harm Bella. He clearly loved her very much."

"I guess we may never find out the truth, now that Calvin is gone," Jason mused.

"I won't give up that easily," Jenny said. "I need to dig deeper."

Jenny's phone beeped just then.

"It's Nick," she said, sounding surprised. "He wants me to open the front door."

Jason followed Jenny out to the foyer and kept an eye on her as she flung the door open.

"Surprise!" Jenny's son Nick stood outside, his arms wide open, ready to fold Jenny into a hug.

Tears streamed down Jenny's eyes as she held on

tightly to her son.

"Hey, hey," Nick said, wiping her tears with his hand. "I thought you'd be happy to see me."

"She's been stressed lately," Jason offered, giving Nick a slap on the back. "She'll be fine now that you're here."

The Magnolias hugged Nick one by one. Nick attacked the pizza with gusto.

"Why didn't you let me know you were coming?" Jenny asked. "I would have cooked something for you."

"You can cook all weekend, Mom," Nick assured her. "I insist."

"We'll have a barbecue, invite everyone." Jason started planning ahead. "The weather's in the high 60s all weekend. Great spring weather."

Nick made quick work of a slice of pizza and scrambled up the stairs to meet Emily.

"Don't wake her up," Jenny called out.

"He won't," Star assured her. "He's so careful with the baby."

"What were you two whispering about in the kitchen?"

Heather asked, never one to miss a beat.

Jenny told her what they had learned about Calvin.

"It's hard to believe someone was out to get him," Heather observed. "I mean, I am sure most people barely spared him a glance."

"He must have antagonized someone," Molly offered. "Maybe Bella wasn't the only one he was stalking. Do you think he was hounding other girls at school?"

"All the pictures I saw in his room were of Bella," Jenny told them. "Maybe she was his current obsession. He might have been fixated on some other girl before this."

"So he had some kind of mania?" Heather asked, looking terrified. "He just went around shadowing people and taking their pictures?"

Nick heard them as he came down the stairs.

"Are you playing Nancy Drew again, Mom?" he asked. "You will be careful, won't you? I worry about you."

"I have plenty of people to take care of me, son," Jenny assured him. "I'll be fine."

"We almost lost you a couple of times," Nick reminded her.

"Let's talk about something else," Betty Sue said. "I am ready for dessert."

Molly had made her special triple chocolate brownies along with homemade fudge. She warmed them up a bit and Jenny scooped vanilla ice cream on top.

"When are you going to use that gift certificate we gave you, Jenny?" Heather asked.

The Magnolias had gifted Jenny a photo session with a famous photographer in Virginia Beach. At the time, Jenny had been set to marry Adam and the Magnolias had assumed the new couple would use it to get some post wedding photos.

"We never got a chance to use it," Jenny said, looking at Jason. "I wouldn't mind taking some pictures with the baby."

Jason's eyes brightened and he grinned from ear to ear.

"Are you serious, Jenny? How about a family photo?"

"You, me and Emily," Jenny murmured.

"And Nick and Star too," Jason added. "We are all a family now."

"Keep us out of it," Star said. "I don't want to be a third wheel."

"I agree," Nick said. "It should be just the happy couple with Emily."

"Why don't we do both?" Jason asked trying to seek middle ground. "We will do one session for all of us, and one for me and Jenny with the baby."

"Let's get some with just the baby," Jenny said, getting excited. "I can put them up in her room."

"How about some shots of the baby with her mama?" Star suggested, her eyes misting over.

"That's a great idea," Jenny nodded. "I can't wait."

"I'll call tomorrow and try to get an appointment for this weekend," Jason said, his eyes bursting with love as he looked at Jenny.

Chapter 13

Jenny's car idled a couple of houses away from Calvin Butler's home. Jenny did a silent recon of the street and inched her car along. Heather was sitting next to her, looking bored, munching noisily on potato chips.

"I don't understand why we are here. Didn't you say Calvin's parents worked in the city?"

"That's exactly what I'm banking on," Jenny said. "They won't be here at this time."

"Are we breaking in?" Heather asked, finally perking up.

"We are doing nothing of the kind," Jenny said firmly.

A loud tapping on the window made Jenny whirl around. An old woman stood outside, holding a walking stick. She waved it menacingly at Jenny and motioned her to open her window.

Jenny took in the craggy face and the heavily wrinkled hands and decided the woman was harmless.

"If you don't beat it in the next two minutes, I'm calling the police," the woman warned.

Her raspy voice told Jenny she meant business.

"We don't mean any harm," Jenny said quickly.

"What are you selling?" the woman demanded as a wracking cough shook her entire body.

"We are friends of Calvin," Heather informed the old woman. "We are here to pay our respects."

"That creepy kid?" the woman grumbled. "You don't look his type."

"He had a type?" Jenny asked, smiling encouragingly at the woman.

She harrumphed and turned around and tottered down the road without a backward glance.

"Are we supposed to follow her?" Heather wondered.

"I don't think so," Jenny said.

She started her car again and ambled along, stopping two houses down. A woman sitting out on a porch smiled and waved at them. Jenny waved back.

"We are getting out here, Heather. Wipe your hands."

Heather dusted off the crumbs from her hands and rubbed them on her jeans before Jenny could pull out a tissue.

"You're worse than Nick," she said, rolling her eyes.

They got out of the car and walked down a small driveway toward the house. Part of the three steps going up to the porch had been converted into a ramp. Paint peeled off a wooden rocking chair and a small table held an old fashioned cordless phone. As they got closer, Jenny noticed the woman was sitting in a wheelchair.

"Hello, hello," she called out cheerfully. "I'm Francine. I've been watching you for the past hour. Are you waiting for someone?"

"Not exactly," Jenny said, reluctant to lie to the woman.

"Well, sit down. Take a load off." Francine urged them.

Heather bagged the rocker and Jenny sat on a bench next to it.

"Can I offer you some tea?" Francine asked eagerly. "You'll have to help me get it though."

"Please don't trouble yourself," Jenny said.

"It's no trouble," Francine said, shaking her head. "I'm a bit parched myself. Come into the kitchen with me. You can bring the tray out."

The woman wheeled herself inside and Jenny followed, not sure if she should offer to help her.

"I get around pretty well in the house," the woman said, anticipating Jenny's dilemma. "A girl comes in to help twice a day, makes sure I'm comfortable."

Jenny opened the refrigerator on Francine's instructions and pulled out a fresh pitcher of tea. There was a plate of cookies covered in plastic wrap. Francine told her to take it out. Jenny spotted a tray on the counter and glasses in a cabinet. She arranged everything on the tray and nodded at Francine. They went out to the porch.

"I've been alone since my Joe passed," Francine told Jenny as she poured the tea.

"It must be tough, living on your own," Jenny commiserated.

"It is what it is," Francine shrugged. "I try to make the best of it. My niece comes in to help and I have learned to do a lot of things on my own over the years."

"Do you drive?" Heather asked impulsively.

Jenny cleared her throat and gave Heather a warning look. Francine didn't seem offended by the question.

"Not anymore," she admitted readily. "I hardly ever

get out these days. This porch right here is my window to the world. I'm so glad spring is here. I can sit out here all day long and entertain myself."

"Really?" Heather asked with a frown. "Looks like a quiet street. You must hardly see anyone."

"You would be surprised," Francine winked. "I see people getting in and out when they are not supposed to, indulging in all kinds of illicit stuff."

Jenny sipped the sweet tea, feeling refreshed. Francine urged them to sample the oatmeal raisin cookies. They were her mother's recipe.

"I can still mix cookie dough," Francine told them.

"Have you heard of the Boardwalk Café?" Jenny asked. "It's my place. Why don't you come over for lunch sometime? Heather or I can come and get you."

Francine beamed at Jenny. She rattled off the names of some of Jenny's popular dishes. She wanted to sample them all when she got to the café.

"I'd be honored to have you over," Jenny told her again.

Francine drained the last of her tea and stared into Jenny's eyes.

"Are you ready to tell me why you are here? Who are

you spying on?"

Jenny told her about Calvin.

"That poor boy," Francine sniffled. "I used to babysit him. He was always a bit of a loner. He seemed to retract into a shell as he got older."

"Did he have any friends?" Jenny asked.

"Hardly," Francine said in a dry tone. "He used to come over to play chess with my Joe. But he stopped doing that. Then he wouldn't even say hello."

"What about his parents?"

"They work in the city. They barely had time for him."

"So no one came over to hang out with him?" Jenny asked.

Francine shook her head.

"What about a girlfriend?" Heather asked.

"He didn't have one, far as I can tell. That's why I was surprised to see that girl."

Jenny sat up in her seat. Francine went on to describe Calvin's visitor. Based on the description, Jenny was pretty sure she was talking about Ashley. The braces sealed it.

"Was she the only one?"

Francine shook her head.

"There was another girl. And a boy too. It was so unlike Calvin. I thought the tide was turning for him. Then he went and took his own life."

Jenny considered telling Francine the truth behind Calvin's death. She decided to say nothing. She didn't want to frighten the poor woman. They chatted for a while before Jenny stood up to leave.

"Don't be a stranger now, you hear?" Francine told her. "Come around any time. I'll be right here."

"Why don't we go see Ashley now?" Heather asked Jenny as they got into the car.

"That's exactly what we are going to do."

Jenny called Sam and got Ashley's address from him. She fed it into the GPS and followed directions. The house wasn't far from Main Street, a small Cape Cod set in a cul-de-sac.

Ashley reclined on a couch in the living room, covered in a rug, her leg propped up on the coffee table. She was happy to see them.

"I'm so bored," she complained. "There's only so much Netflix I can watch. Give me the latest scoop."

"Are you feeling better?" Jenny asked her solicitously. "How's the pain?"

Ashley brushed their concerns aside. She wanted to talk about Calvin.

"He was voted Most Likely to Commit Suicide, you know," Ashley said with a nasty note creeping into her voice. "I'm not surprised he took his life."

"Did he hang out with you?" Jenny asked.

"Not exactly," Ashley giggled. "He followed Bella around like a puppy. She barely noticed him though."

"Who invited him to the party?" Heather asked.

"I dunno," Ashley shrugged. "It wasn't exactly 'invite only'. Anyone could get in."

"He was right behind you when you crashed your car. Did you know that?"

Ashley shook her head.

"Didn't I tell you? None of us talked to that guy. You could say he was invisible."

"Then what were you doing at his house, Ashley?" Heather challenged. "Someone saw you, so don't try to deny it."

Ashley bit her lip and muttered something under her breath.

"I went there with Olivia."

"Olivia?" Jenny burst out. "I thought you didn't get along."

"We don't," Ashley said bitterly.

"Why would you go anywhere with her then?" Heather asked.

"Olivia saw me with Jake. She threatened to tell Bella I was trying to steal him back."

"Were you?" Jenny asked.

Ashley's eyes grew wide.

"Uh-Uh! Jake and I are done. He broke my heart the day he dumped me for Bella."

"What were you afraid of then?" Jenny asked.

"I ran into Jake at the Creamery. We were just standing there, eating ice cream. Olivia saw us and took a photo."

"Bella would have trusted you," Jenny said. "You were best friends."

"Bella was a sweetie pie," Ashley sighed, "but she was

very possessive when it came to Jake."

"What did Olivia want with Calvin?" Heather asked.

"I don't know," Ashley told them. "He took her down to the basement while I waited in the living room. They were gone for quite a while."

"You didn't try to snoop?" Heather asked, giving Ashley an encouraging smile. "You can tell us."

Ashley leaned forward and nodded quickly.

"I tried. But I couldn't hear anything at first. Then I heard raised voices. Olivia was fuming when she came back up."

"What were they fighting about?" Jenny asked.

"She didn't say. She was pretty nasty on the way back."

"You said Calvin was invisible to you," Heather mused. "How did you know where he lived?"

"Calvin wasn't always a nerd," Ashley said. "Our mothers were friends. We had a lot of play dates growing up. Then they moved to a bigger house. Calvin's mother got a job in the city. My mom says she got all high and mighty after that." Ashley seemed miserable as she reminisced about her childhood. "I guess we just grew apart."

"What do you think Olivia wanted with Calvin?" Jenny asked.

"Who can tell with her?" Ashley quipped. "It was probably some plan to make Bella look bad."

An alarm went off somewhere inside the house. An elderly nurse appeared and reminded Ashley to take her pills.

"Time to leave now, ladies," she said. "Ashley needs her rest."

Jenny and Heather wished Ashley a speedy recovery and filed out.

"Do you think she's lying?" Jenny asked Heather as she started the car.

"This is all too much to take in, Jenny," Heather moaned. "And I'm starving. Lunch was hours ago."

"I can fix you a sandwich when we get home," Jenny offered.

"Why don't we go to Ethan's Crab Shack? A basket of fried fish sounds good to me right now."

Jenny's face fell.

Ethan Hopkins was Adam's brother. Once a regular visitor to his fish and chips shop, Jenny had avoided him like the plague since the wedding.

"What's Ethan done to you, huh?" Heather grumbled. "Are you never going to eat there again?"

"It's too soon," Jenny said glumly. "Can we go somewhere else?"

"Forget it," Heather said, tearing open a packet of pretzels.

"It's not like you are starving," Jenny said primly. "You seem to have emptied the snacks aisle at the grocery store."

Heather ignored her and started talking about Ashley.

"If you ask me, she's still the top suspect in Bella's death. What was all that about Olivia, though?"

"Do you think Ashley and Olivia hatched something together?" Jenny wondered out loud. "I think they both despised Bella. Ashley just wasn't open about it."

"Olivia could have been working with Calvin," Heather suggested. "We can't be sure why he followed Bella around. If she wasn't too nice to him, he might have been planning something against her."

"Calvin's not here to defend himself," Jenny reminded Heather. "So we'll have to go back to the other two."

Chapter 14

Jenny placed a batch of strawberry muffins in the oven. The Boardwalk Café was bursting at the seams with tourists hungry for their breakfast. The Eastern Shore was enjoying a warm spring and many people from the north had traveled down to take advantage of it.

The Magnolias sat at their usual table on the deck outside, arguing over the upcoming film festival.

"I still think the film festival should not be clubbed with the Spring Fest," Star was saying strongly.

"Do you have a compelling argument against it?" Betty Sue asked her. "You know how Barb is when she gets hold of an idea."

Heather moaned in delight as she tasted a strawberry muffin hot from the oven.

"These are amazing, Jenny," she crooned. "The citrus flavor just bursts in your mouth."

"It's the orange zest," Jenny told her, blushing lightly at the praise. "It works well with the strawberries."

"Have you decided which sundae you are making for

the festival?" Molly asked.

"I'm going with the strawberry shortcake," Jenny told her.

"These muffins would be great for the festival too," Betty Sue said, taking a bite.

She finished her muffin in a few bites and asked Jenny about Calvin.

"Anything new about that poor boy?"

Jenny's forehead creased into a frown. She gave a slight shrug.

"Calvin was a loner alright. But many people seem to have visited him in the last few days of his life. I wonder why."

"But if he didn't take his own life, what happened to him?"

"I think we are dealing with a clever criminal here," Jenny said, pinching her lip. "Maybe this was the plan all along. This person got Bella out of the way first. Then they staged Calvin's death, trying to pin the blame on him. They wanted it to look like a murder-suicide."

"Who else knew about Calvin's obsession with Bella?" Molly wanted to know.

"They all knew," Heather said expansively. "The kids, I mean. This kind of thing doesn't stay hidden in a high school."

"Are you saying one of the kids is behind all this?" Jenny asked, wide eyed. "They are just teenagers, Heather."

"That's right," Heather said grimly. "Teenagers, not toddlers. They are smart enough to devise a plan and see it through."

"I need to find out more about Olivia," Jenny said. "Where was she on the day of the accident?"

"We should go talk to her," Heather said eagerly. "I'm done with all my chores at the inn. I'm free for the rest of the day."

"I wish someone else could tell us about Olivia," Jenny mused. "I'd rather not ask her."

"What about him?" Molly asked, pointing to a large figure ambling along the beach.

Sam heaved himself over the stairs and greeted Jenny, slightly out of breath.

"I was craving your seafood chowder," he said. "Any chance I can have some?"

"I'm not making chowder today," Jenny told him,

pursing her mouth. "It's a bit early for lunch anyway. Would you like to try some strawberry muffins?"

Sam pulled up a chair at a nearby table and flopped down in it. He nodded eagerly, wiping the sweat off his forehead with the back of his hand.

Betty Sue glared at him, her eyes full of disdain. Heather patted her and stood up.

"Time for us to go, I think. I'll join you later, Jenny."

The Magnolias cleared out one by one. Star went into the kitchen to help Jenny prep for lunch. Jenny brought out a plate with four muffins and a crock of butter. She fully expected Sam to ask for a second helping.

Sam swallowed the first two muffins and came up for air after the third one.

"Yummy," he crooned, a smile of satisfaction lighting up his face. "Can I have more?"

Jenny obliged him and brought out another plate.

"Are you on a diet?" Jenny asked him.

"Don't need to be," Sam beamed, his mouth covered in crumbs.

He barely looked up as Jenny sat down before him,

engrossed in generously buttering each muffin before he popped it in his mouth.

"Say, you know Olivia, don't you?"

Sam nodded with his mouth full.

"Was she at Bella's party?"

Sam mumbled something, spraying a few muffin crumbs from his mouth around Jenny.

"She wasn't invited?" Jenny asked, trying not to flinch.

Sam shook his head, a sneer spreading across his face.

"That didn't stop her though. She crashed the party with some guy."

"How did that go with Bella?"

"Not well, as you can imagine." Sam finally slid his empty plate forward and wiped his mouth with a napkin. "Bella was sure she was there to make trouble."

"Why? Did Olivia do something?"

"Bella asked her to clear out," Sam said, rubbing his chest. "You don't have anything for heartburn, do you?"

Jenny shook her head.

"They got into it alright, those two," Sam continued. "Bella told her to get lost."

"I'm guessing Olivia didn't go quietly?"

"She threatened Bella," Sam nodded. "She told her she would be sorry."

"Do you think she meant to harm Bella?" Jenny asked, alert.

"I think she was going to tattle to her uncle," Sam dismissed. "That's what she did all the time. That's exactly why Bella didn't want her at the party."

"What happened after this fight?"

"She left," Sam shrugged. "Dragged that guy along with her."

"Do you know where they went?"

"I heard something about the Rusty Anchor," Sam said, scratching his head. "But I can't be sure."

Sam wanted some milk to wash the muffins down. Jenny brought out a tall glass for him. He drained it in a couple of gulps and was gone before Jenny could ask him anything else.

The lunch hour kept Jenny busy. She finally sat down with Star to eat a bite herself.

"What is your next move?" Star asked.

"I am going to meet Mr. Worthington again."

Jenny called Heather and told her to be ready. She picked her up an hour later and they were soon driving into the hills toward the Worthington house. Jenny had secured an appointment with Bella's father.

They were ushered into a formal living room. Max Worthington sat under a big portrait of Bella, tapping his foot impatiently.

"I hope you are not here to waste my time," he grumbled, glancing at his watch. "I had to drop something important to come and meet you here."

"It will be worth your while," Jenny promised.

"Get on with it then."

"How much wealth does Olivia inherit now that Bella is gone?" Jenny got straight to the point.

"Olivia?" Max asked incredulously. "She doesn't get a dime."

It was Jenny's turn to be surprised.

"Isn't Olivia the next of kin now? I thought she would be your heir?"

"Olivia is my brother's step daughter," Max explained. "The Worthington fortune can only be inherited by someone who shares our bloodline. My great grandfather made sure of that in his will."

"Does Olivia know that?" Jenny asked.

Max shrugged.

"I don't know what my brother has told her. She won't be penniless, of course. She will have enough to live comfortably. But she won't be the heiress my Bella was."

He stood up and paced around the room impatiently. Then he sat down and looked at Jenny.

"You don't think Olivia would hurt my Isabella, do you?"

His eyes had turned red and he pinched the bridge of his nose, looking deflated. He let out a soft groan and stared at Jenny with a bewildered expression.

"If Olivia wanted money, she just had to ask. Surely you don't think she killed my Bella for that?"

"I don't know," Jenny admitted. "That's what I am trying to find out."

"What about that boy?" Max asked suddenly. "Olivia told me all about him."

"Do you mean Sam?"

"Not that greedy pig! This slacker my baby wanted to marry."

"Jake," Jenny nodded. "What about him?"

"I know nothing about him. He's just a bum, isn't he? I say he wanted Bella's money for himself."

"How would he have access to your fortune?" Jenny asked.

"Bella had a big trust fund from her mother's family. She got full control of it when she turned 18. You know what I just found out? It's all going to this kid."

"What?" Jenny exclaimed.

"That's right," Max said, clenching his fists. "I am going to inform the police about this."

"Jake loved Bella," Jenny reasoned. "He wouldn't harm her for a few dollars."

"Make that several million," Max smirked. He stood up and started walking out of the room. "I need to get back to the office."

Jenny understood they were being dismissed.

"Thank you for meeting me at such short notice," she

partner

said. "We can see ourselves out."

Jenny was a bit dazed as she processed the latest information Max had provided.

"Don't you see, Jenny?" Heather asked excitedly as Jenny started driving back to the café. "Bella's father knew about her engagement."

"Did you see the look in his eyes?" Jenny asked. "He's grieving for his daughter, Heather."

"Don't get sentimental, Jenny," Heather scoffed. "He might be repenting now, after the fact. How do you know he didn't get into a rage when he found out what Bella was up to?"

"We need to talk to Jake again," Jenny said, narrowing her eyes. "I wonder if we can find him on the beach."

Jake was lying on the beach in the same spot where Jenny had met him earlier. With dark shades covering his eyes and his arms around his head, he looked like he didn't have a care in the world.

Jenny stood before him with her hands on her hips, forcing him to get up.

"What do you want now?" he asked, stifling a yawn.

"Did you have a fight with Bella?" Jenny asked. "Is that why you didn't drop her home?"

"I wouldn't call it a fight," Jake said reluctantly. "It was our special night. I wanted Bella to stay there longer. But she went on and on about her curfew."

"Word around here is you are too lazy," Heather said. "I guess you couldn't be bothered to leave the party to see your fiancée home."

"I wanted to," Jake said earnestly, taking his shades off.

Jenny searched for dishonesty in his clear blue eyes.

"Bella wouldn't listen," Jake continued. "And I was pretty drunk myself. So I didn't push it."

"You were all drunk," Jenny snapped. "Why was it okay for Ashley to drive her?"

"I thought the driver would take Bella home," Jake said meekly. "I never went out to see her off." His eyes filled up suddenly. "If I had seen Ashley get into the driver's seat, I might have stopped them. But I didn't want to leave the party."

Jenny was saving the best for last.

"When did Bella tell you she was leaving you all her money?"

"She didn't," Jake said, looking surprised. "Why would she do that?"

"Everyone knows you can't be bothered to lift a finger," Heather said. "Now you can take Bella's money and go gallivanting around Europe on your own."

"I don't want Bella's money, okay?" Jake said, incensed. "So I like to play it cool. That doesn't mean I'm a total bum. I'm going to night school."

"Really?" Jenny asked, quirking an eyebrow.

"Bella and I planned to go to the same college after we got back from Europe."

Jenny felt sorry for the boy.

"You can still do that," she said kindly. "It's what Bella would want."

"Yes," Jake said, staring at his feet. "She always wanted the best for me. She made me believe in myself again, you know."

Jenny patted him on the shoulder and turned around to go back to the café. Heather followed her with a frown.

"You can't believe everything he says," she reminded Jenny. "Bella was glued to him all evening. He could easily have slipped something in her drink."

Jenny wove her arm into Heather's and gave her a

sympathetic look.

"Have you stopped believing in love?"

Chapter 15

The Magnolias huddled together at their favorite table on the deck of the Boardwalk Café. A bank of clouds had moved in during the night and the rain had kept up since early morning. It had taken away some of the warmth of the spring day.

"Stop acting like a child," Betty Sue told Star, her hands busy knitting a violet scarf. "I don't see what the problem is."

Jenny poured some coffee for herself and observed her aunt over the rim of her coffee cup. She tried to reason with her.

"You have spent almost every evening with Jimmy for several months. This doesn't have to be different."

Star muttered to herself, refusing to stop doodling on a paper napkin.

"He's making it so. Don't you see?"

"What did he say, exactly?" Betty Sue asked.

Star tried to hide a blush.

"Jimmy says he wants the evening to be special. He's

taking me to The Steakhouse."

The Steakhouse was fancy and expensive, the only such restaurant in Pelican Cove. Going to the Steakhouse was a sure way to inform everyone that you were celebrating something special.

"Wow!" Molly beamed. "That sounds big. Do you think he will propose?"

Star sprang back in her seat.

"He better not do that. I am not ready."

"You've got one foot in the grave," Betty Sue told her. "What are you waiting for?"

"Speak for yourself," Star grumbled at her. "I'm barely seventy."

"I think it's cute," Heather laughed, nibbling on a cupcake. "You are already acting like a blushing bride. We might have another wedding to plan soon."

"Don't get ideas, girlie," Star snapped. "Not unless you are ready to stand at the altar with your latest boyfriend."

"I'm having a dry spell," Heather said with a shrug. "Slim pickings around here. You should hang on to Jimmy with all you've got."

Star's agitation increased as Heather talked.

"Give it a rest," Jenny warned her friend. "Can't you see how upset she is?"

"Get a hold of yourself, Star," Betty Sue said kindly. "What's the worst that can happen? He will say he loves you. You already know that."

"It's evident to anyone who's seen you together," Molly nodded in affirmation.

"I know it and he knows it," Star agreed. "But neither of us has ever said it out loud."

Jenny took her aunt's hand in hers. She didn't like to see her so flustered.

"What is it that you are afraid of?"

"It's going to change everything," Star sighed. "Things won't be the same."

"I'm sure Jimmy won't rush you into anything," Jenny said. "He's pretty laid back that way."

"It will change everything," Star said again.

"Change is good," Heather piped up. "Change is the one constant in our life."

"That's enough, Heather," Betty Sue chided. She

looked sympathetically at her friend. "You are all anxious now, Star, but I am sure you will feel better tomorrow."

"What if he gives me an ultimatum?" Star voiced her concern. "All or nothing?"

"Is that what you are afraid of?" Jenny asked, suddenly realizing why her aunt was so frantic with worry. "Jimmy won't do that, Star."

"Stop overthinking this," Molly said firmly. "Just put on a nice dress and enjoy your evening."

"You can be sure of one thing," Betty Sue said, putting her knitting down. "We will be here for you no matter what."

"That's right," Jenny agreed. "You've got us."

"For better or for worse," Heather quipped.

The Magnolias clasped each other's hands, finally making Star smile.

The rain was coming down harder. Molly looked across the deserted beach and clucked in exasperation.

"This day is turning out to be too depressing. I don't feel like going back to work."

"Why don't we go out tonight?" Heather suggested.

"It's been a while."

The girls agreed to meet at the Rusty Anchor later that evening. Jenny got busy with the lunch prep after the Magnolias left. She made French Onion soup and fried fish sandwiches. The café was almost deserted so Jenny convinced Star to go home early.

"Grab some beauty sleep and take a nice hot bath," she told her aunt. "Use those lavender bath salts I gave you for Christmas."

"It's just dinner with Jimmy," Star protested. "I'm not going to primp."

Jenny flung up her arms in frustration, refusing to respond to her aunt.

Jenny prepped for the next day and finally sat down to enjoy a last cup of coffee before closing up. Her thoughts turned to Bella and she tried to make sense of all the information she had gathered until then. Was she missing something obvious?

Jenny was looking forward to letting her hair down and relaxing with her friends by the time evening rolled around. Molly and Heather were waiting for her at the Rusty Anchor.

"Chris can't get away from the market," she told Jenny.

"Jason's busy too," Jenny told her. "I guess it's just us

girls then."

"Thank God for that," Heather said loudly. "I do not enjoy being the fifth wheel all the time."

Eddie Cotton, the bar owner, brought them a round of drinks along with a bowl of pretzels. Jenny remembered what she wanted to ask him.

"Can you spare a minute, Eddie?" she asked.

"Are you detecting again, Jenny?" he asked indulgently.

"Sort of," Jenny admitted readily. "Do you know a young girl called Olivia? I want to know if she came here on a certain day."

"You mean the Worthington girl?" Eddie asked. "Sure. She comes here a lot with a young fella."

Jenny told him the date of Bella's party. Eddie wasn't sure he could remember back to that day.

"She's here right now, in case you wanted to talk to her," Eddie said, pointing his thumb at a small corner table.

Jenny peered through the dimly lit room and spotted Olivia. She was draining a glass of beer and talking softly to a man.

"Thanks," she told Eddie. "I think I will go say hello."

Jenny walked over to Olivia's table without giving much thought to what she wanted to ask her. The man sitting at her table said something to Olivia and left without a second glance at Jenny.

Jenny decided to take the bull by the horns.

"Why did you crash Bella's party?"

Olivia looked up and stared at Jenny with a puzzled frown. Then her face cleared and her eyes narrowed in recognition.

"You came to visit my uncle, right? What do you want?"

"I want to know why you hated Bella," Jenny said, her hands on her hips. "What did you have against her?"

"I didn't hate Bella," Olivia dismissed.

"You sneaked up on her and snitched on her. You got her in trouble with her father."

"Bella was a brat!" Olivia spat. "I was just looking out for her."

"By having her sent to some correctional school?"

"Bella was into drugs," Olivia said with a shrug. "She needed to be reigned in."

"Did you think her father would write her off and leave all his wealth to you?" Heather asked.

She had followed Jenny to Olivia's table.

"He doesn't have a choice," Olivia said smugly. "I'm the next in line to inherit."

"You won't get a penny," Heather told her. "Mr. Worthington told us so."

Olivia's smile faltered. She finally lost her cool.

"Who are you, anyway? Why are you asking me all these questions?"

"Jenny's going to find out what happened to Bella," Heather replied. "You won't get away easily."

"Just leave me alone," Olivia screeched.

"Do you prefer talking to the police?" Jenny asked. "Why did you go to Bella's party?"

"I heard she was getting engaged, okay? I wanted to see it for myself."

"So you could report back to your uncle?" Jenny quizzed. "Why did you fight with Bella that night?"

"I don't remember," Olivia said. "We quarreled a lot." She took another sip of her drink and seemed to come to a decision. "Look, I was hoping to discredit Bella. She made it really easy with her wild lifestyle. I didn't grow up rich like her. My father stayed away from the family business, did an ordinary government job on a meager salary. I didn't know how much I had missed until I came to work for my uncle."

"You wanted to grab everything you had missed out on," Jenny summed up.

"Why shouldn't I?" Olivia asked. "I'm a Worthington too."

Jenny thought about what Max had told them about Olivia's parentage. Either Olivia was unaware of her roots or she was in denial.

"Judging by all accounts, there was plenty to go around," Jenny reasoned. "Did you have to get Bella out of the way?"

"I hated her," Olivia said glibly. "I wanted to see her squirm."

"I wouldn't say things like that if I were you," Heather observed.

"I'm just being honest," Olivia shrugged. "I admit I wanted her gone. But I would never harm her."

"What did you do after Bella threw you out that night?"

"She didn't throw me out, okay?" Olivia grumbled. "I came here."

"Can anyone vouch for that?" Jenny asked.

"Plenty of people," Olivia told her. "There was a trivia contest here that night. I played and I won. I am sure many people will remember that."

"Probably," Jenny conceded.

Olivia took a sip of water and seemed to simmer down.

"Look, you've got it all wrong. I am not the one you should be focusing on."

Jenny raised her eyebrows and twisted her mouth in a grimace.

"Who did you have in mind?"

"Ashley, of course," Olivia said quickly. "You know that pudgy girl with a mouthful of crooked teeth?"

Olivia's description of Ashley may have been unkind but it was spot on.

"I know who Ashley is," Jenny said sharply. "She is at home, convalescing. Did you know she was badly hurt in the accident?"

Olivia rolled her eyes.

"So she's playing the victim?"

"What do you have against that poor girl?" Heather burst out, settling into the seat in front of Olivia.

"She's a crafty one," Olivia said dourly. "She wanted every little thing Bella had. Copied what she did right down to the shade of lip gloss she wore."

"Friends do that," Jenny said with a shrug. "She's blaming herself for the accident."

"It's all an act," Olivia insisted. "Do you know what she was doing at that party? Taking bets on how long Bella's engagement would last."

"I don't see Ashley doing that," Jenny dismissed.

"I was right there," Olivia reminded her. "Take my word for it."

Jenny remembered her conversation with Calvin's neighbor. She took a shot in the dark.

"If you are so set against Ashley, what were you doing hanging out with her? Why did you go to Calvin Butler's house with Ashley?"

Olivia's nostrils flared and her cheeks flamed.

"I don't know what you mean."

"Don't try to deny it," Jenny warned. "How did you know Calvin?"

Olivia's shoulders slumped. She exhaled noisily and began tearing a paper napkin into shreds.

"It was Ashley's idea," she said softly. "She said there was this nerd who was mad about Bella."

"Go on," Jenny prompted.

"We wanted him to do something …" Olivia looked troubled. "We just wanted Bella to break up with Jake, that's all."

"You couldn't bear seeing her happy, could you?" Heather accused.

Olivia nodded.

"I wanted to give Bella a reality check. Ashley was possessive about Jake."

"So you convinced Calvin to get Bella out of the picture?" Jenny gasped.

"He was just going to make sure they broke up," Olivia insisted.

She had lost all her bluster. Jenny felt sorry for her.

"Looks like things got horribly out of hand."

Chapter 16

It was a momentous day for the new family. Jenny and Jason were taking Emily for her first haircut. When Emily came to Jason at a few months old, she had been almost bald with the finest wispy brown hair covering her head. Her hair had begun to grow after she turned eight months old. Now at fourteen months, her hair was beginning to get into her eyes and hung below her neck. Jenny had tried to trim it a bit at home a couple of months ago. Her efforts had been amateurish at best and it showed.

Jenny gazed delightedly at the clear blue skies and clutched Jason's hand in excitement. They both turned around in their seats to look at Emily.

Emily smiled at them from her car seat and waved her hands.

"Dada, Dada ..." she cried with wide eyes.

"Are you ready, baby?" Jason asked his daughter. "We're getting your first haircut."

"Shhh ..." Jenny warned. "Don't call it that. You might scare her."

"I'm not sure she even understands me, Jenny," Jason

laughed.

They had an appointment at a special salon in the neighboring town. Jenny had heard about it from one of the café's customers. She had fixed an appointment right away and pushed Jason to take a day off from work.

"We have done everything on this checklist," Jenny muttered, reading off her phone. "She's had her snack and she just had a nap. She should be good to go."

A young, chirpy girl greeted them effusively when they reached the salon. Emily was given a tiny teddy bear to play with. She burst into smiles but raised a fuss when the stylist tried to tie the cape around her.

"I brought an old shirt she can wear," Jenny said, pulling the garment out of her bag.

Jason asked her to pose with Emily for a 'before' picture. Jenny and Jason both kept the baby entertained while the stylist began snipping at her hair. Just when Jenny noticed Emily's eyes begin to droop, the stylist announced she was done. More pictures followed and Emily was given a special certificate for successfully completing her first haircut.

"This is our baby's first trophy," Jenny said, her eyes shining. "Sort of."

"We need to celebrate," Jason said, scooping his

daughter up into his arms. "Let's get some burgers and shakes."

Jason took them to a well known diner that was famous for serving the best cheeseburgers on the Eastern Shore.

Jenny couldn't stop taking pictures of the baby while they waited for their food to arrive.

"Her mother should have been with her today," Jenny clucked.

"You *are* her mother, Jenny," Jason comforted her. "You're the only mother Emily's ever known."

"We'll have to tell her one day," Jenny said heavily.

"Not anytime soon," Jason said. "Let's not worry about it now."

Jason dropped Jenny off at the café and took Emily home. Jenny was in a peculiar mood as she prepped for the next day. Heather had come around to help her.

"How was your day with Emily?" she asked Jenny.

"Emily was a dear. She didn't fuss at all."

"Then what are you brooding about, Jenny? You don't look happy."

"I can't stop thinking about Bella," Jenny admitted. "We talked to so many people but I'm nowhere near figuring out who might be involved. I'm going around in circles."

"I have a suggestion but you are not going to like it."

"Don't even think about it," Jenny sizzled. "There's no way I am going to talk to that scoundrel Adam. I don't want him mentioned in my presence."

"You'll have to make your peace with him, you know," Heather reasoned. "You can't avoid each other forever. Not in a place as small as Pelican Cove."

"I'll find a way," Jenny grimaced.

The two friends worked silently for a while, trying to avoid arguing over a hot button topic. Jenny started a fresh pot of coffee and set out some chocolate chip cookies to go with it.

"Calvin must have known something," she mused. "Why else would someone want him out of the way?"

"You don't think he actually harmed Bella?" Heather asked.

"Let's say he did," Jenny said. "Who would want him out of the way?"

"Someone who loved Bella," Heather said. "You think

Calvin's murder was revenge for what he did?"

"Doesn't that sound extreme?" Jenny asked Heather. "Only someone obsessed with Bella would take such a drastic step. Calvin's actions were almost fanatic. Jake supposedly loved Bella but I don't think he's the type to go after retribution."

"That poor Calvin," Heather sighed. "I don't know if he was guilty. But I can't help but feel sorry for him."

"Do you think he went investigating on his own and found something?" Jenny asked.

"And he was silenced before he could notify anyone?" Heather asked. "That sounds possible."

"And he was killed in his own house," Jenny said, rubbing a gold charm that hung around her neck.

Her son Nick had gifted her a charm for Mother's Day every year since he turned eight. Jenny wore them around her neck on a thin gold chain. She had a habit of rubbing the charms whenever she was worried about something or thinking of her son.

"He was killed in his own house, Heather," Jenny repeated urgently. "Why didn't I think of this before?"

Heather waited for her to go on.

"Calvin must have known this person," Jenny finished

triumphantly.

"He actually let them in," Heather cried, catching on.

"That's right," Jenny added. "That means he didn't suspect this person at all."

"Or he was trying to be clever," Heather said softly. "And his plan backfired."

"Who was Calvin friendly with?" Jenny asked. "Let's make a list."

"Not many people," Heather said, stalling her. "He was the school nerd, remember? Hardly anyone spoke to him."

"Ashley knew him," Jenny reminded her. "So did Sam. I bet Jake knew him too."

"Ashley can't get around," Heather reminded Jenny. "Does that mean Sam or Jake went over to his house?"

"Wait a minute," Jenny said, holding up a hand. "Let's not forget Olivia. She admitted she went over to Calvin's with Ashley."

"We need to find out what they talked about," Heather said. "What exactly was Calvin going to do to nix Bella's engagement?"

"Is that really important?" Jenny asked. "We know he

wasn't successful."

"That might have angered him," Heather said. "Making him harm Bella."

"Are we back to that again?" Jenny asked in frustration.

"Can we try to simplify all this?" Heather asked.

"Either Calvin was guilty of the first crime or he wasn't," Jenny reasoned. "Let's say he wasn't. He must have found out who hurt Bella. In that case, he was silenced before he could raise the alarm about this person."

"That does seem to be the strongest theory," Heather acknowledged.

"We need to focus on Bella then," Jenny summed up.

"We already talked to most of the people at the party," Heather said.

"Did we really?" Jenny wondered, draining her coffee cup.

She tapped some keys on her phone and dialed Ashley. Jenny rushed through the niceties and asked for Sam's address. She dumped some cookies in a paper bag after she hung up and grabbed her bag.

"Let's go," she said, hustling Heather out.

Jenny drove to a part of town she had never been to before. She guided her car along a dirt road in a wooded area. The tall firs towered over them, creating a canopy that blocked most of the sunlight. Jenny gritted her teeth as the car shuddered on the uneven ground. The road turned one last time and brought them to a big clearing.

A couple of rundown trailers were parked before them, looking deserted. Jenny and Heather got out and looked around, trying to see some sign of life. A couple of camp chairs and a trestle table were set outside one of the trailers. Jenny walked purposefully toward them and rapped loudly on the trailer. The door opened just a crack and a familiar face peered out.

Sam looked astonished as he stared at them. He squeezed out of the half open door, taking care to open it as little as possible. Jenny's hand flew to cover her nose as a vile stench escaped from the trailer. She spied a sink full of dirty dishes and a small counter top stacked high with empty food cartons and cereal boxes.

"Let's sit here," Sam said, pointing to the two chairs.

He looked uncharacteristically flustered. Ketchup and mustard stains were splattered across his grimy shirt.

He reeked of a disgusting mixture of deodorant and sweat. Jenny wondered when he had last taken a bath.

"Ashley told us where to find you," Jenny explained. "I hope we are not disturbing you?"

"I don't like to bring people here," Sam said sheepishly. "I guess you can see why."

"Do you live here with your family?" Heather asked.

Sam gave a mirthless laugh.

"I don't have one," he said with a shrug. "I'm on my own."

Jenny handed over the bag of cookies she had brought with her. Sam surprised her by setting it on the table without a second glance.

"Don't you get lonely out here?" Jenny asked Sam.

"I don't have a choice," Sam said. "I was a foster kid. I hardly remember my birth parents. I have been on my own since I aged out of the system."

"Don't you have a job?" Heather asked condescendingly. "You can get a cheap room in town, you know."

"Bella took care of me," Sam said fiercely. "She was the sister I never had."

Heather and Jenny exchanged a glance. Sam had probably been living off Bella's generosity all this time.

Tears were flowing down Sam's cheeks. He wiped them with the back of his hand.

"Do you have any new information?" he begged. "Please tell me you haven't given up."

"Don't worry, Sam," Jenny assured him. "I am not ready to throw in the towel yet."

"We are here to ask you some questions," Heather prompted, trying to steer the conversation toward the purpose of their visit.

"That's right," Jenny nodded. "Do you have any pictures from Bella's engagement party?"

Sam pulled his phone out of his pocket.

"I did take some photos," he told them. "But most of them show the happy couple."

"Never mind that," Jenny said. "Just let me have a look."

She took the phone Sam held out and flipped through the images. Although Bella and Jake were highlighted in most of the photos, Sam had unwittingly captured people in the background. Jenny pointed at a few unfamiliar faces and asked Sam who they were. Most of them were kids from Bella's school. Jenny spotted Calvin lurking in a corner in many of the photos. There were some group shots with Ashley and Sam. Then she spotted Olivia in one of the pictures.

"How long was Olivia at the party?" she asked Sam. "Didn't Bella have a fight with her?"

"Bella threw her out," Sam grinned. "She could be quite gutsy when she wanted to be."

"Who's that guy?" Jenny asked, peering at a young man who was definitely not a highschooler.

Sam scratched his nose and shook his head.

"I don't know. He must have been someone's date."

"Looks kind of old, doesn't he?" Jenny asked.

"He could be someone's big brother," Sam laughed, making a feeble joke.

"Times may have changed," Heather snorted. "But I'm sure high school girls don't bring their brothers to a party."

She looked at the picture again.

"I've seen this guy somewhere."

"Where?" Jenny asked urgently. "Think hard,

Heather."

Heather trained her eyes on the picture and shook her head.

"I'm drawing a blank right now. Maybe it will come to me later."

Jenny grabbed Heather's arm and stared at her grimly.

"We need to find this guy and talk to him, Heather. He could be our missing link."

Chapter 17

Jenny greeted her first customer of the day with a wide smile.

"How are you, Captain Charlie?"

The old salt chatted with her for a while. Jenny offered him her latest creation, a savory muffin made with sundried tomatoes and cheese. Captain Charlie reluctantly agreed to try one.

Jenny made bacon and cheddar omelets for the breakfast crowd. The warmer weather was bringing in more tourists each day. Jenny was surprised to see Sam sitting at a table near the window. He seemed to have cleaned up since their last visit.

"You're up awfully early," she greeted, placing a cup of coffee before him.

"Can we talk?" Sam asked, looking around furtively.

"I'm a bit busy right now," Jenny apologized. "Can you wait until the crowd lets up?"

Sam agreed readily.

"I'll fix you something to eat," Jenny promised.

Sam's face brightened and he rubbed his hands in glee.

"Don't you think I've lost weight?"

Jenny gave him a onceover and held back her response. She thought Sam had put on at least ten pounds since their trip to the mountains.

"Are you on some new diet?" she asked.

"It's not a diet," Sam beamed. "It's a complete weight loss system. It's going to be revolutionary."

"Did you buy it on the Internet?"

"Can't talk about it now," Sam said. "It's top secret."

"Okay," Jenny said with a shrug. "I'll bring your food out in a minute."

Being familiar with Sam's hearty appetite, Jenny loaded his plate with two servings of everything. Sam's eyes shone when Jenny placed the large platter of food before him.

Star arrived an hour later, finally allowing Jenny to take a break.

"What's the matter, Sam?" Jenny asked, pulling up a chair before him.

She handed him a napkin, pointing at a smear of sauce

on his face.

"It's the photos," Sam said, giving his mouth a good scrub with a wad of tissues. "I think I know who that guy is."

"You do?" Jenny asked, leaning forward eagerly.

"Olivia brought him to the party," Sam told her. "I was so focused on that scene between the girls, I kind of forgot about him."

"But who is he. Do you know?"

"I guess he's her boyfriend," Sam shrugged. "I've seen him with her a couple of times."

"Is he from around here?"

"I don't think so," Sam said with a frown. "But he comes to town a lot."

"You didn't remember his name by any chance?"

"Hank. Olivia calls him Hank."

"What else do you know about him?"

"He's some kind of salesman," Sam said uncertainly. "Look, I have to get to school."

Jenny thanked Sam for the information and waved him off. She debated calling Olivia to ask her about her boyfriend.

"You've been holding out on me, Jenny," Heather accused as she swept into the café. "I just met Jason on my way here."

"Did he show you the baby's photos?" Jenny asked indulgently. "Jason's been pulling those pictures out every chance he gets."

"Emily looks cute," Heather declared. "You should enter one of those mother-daughter contests. You are absolutely adorable."

Jenny brought Heather up to speed on Sam's visit.

"So he was keeping this from us," Heather inferred.

"Forget about Sam," Jenny said. "How do we find out more about this Hank?"

"Go to the horse," Heather replied. "Let's go see Olivia."

"I need to get lunch going, Heather."

Olivia surprised them by walking in. She was dressed for the beach, with a large hat on her head and a filmy cover up over her swimsuit and shorts.

She twirled her sunglasses and looked around with a smirk on her face.

"Hello Olivia," Jenny greeted her.

Olivia ignored the greeting, acting like they had never met before.

"Does this joint serve anything cold?"

"We have iced tea and lemonade," Jenny offered.

"No mocktails with those little paper umbrellas?" Olivia sneered.

"I can crush some strawberries and add them to your lemonade," Jenny offered.

"Don't bother," Olivia dismissed. "I'll take two large lemonades to go. Make sure they are ice cold."

"Why don't you wait here while I get your drinks?" Jenny asked smoothly.

Heather bristled with barely controlled anger. She pounced on Olivia as soon as Jenny went inside.

"Looks like your mama didn't teach you any manners."

Olivia didn't take the bait. Jenny came back out before Heather could say anything more.

"Here you go," Jenny said. "Are you spending the day with Hank?"

"What do you know about Hank?" Olivia asked

guardedly.

"He's your beau, isn't he?" Jenny smiled.

Olivia swore under her breath.

"This is why I hate small towns. There is absolutely no privacy here."

"You do spend a lot of time with him," Jenny bluffed. "And he's a handsome devil. People notice, you know."

Olivia relented a bit.

"I guess Hank's kind of attractive."

Heather jumped into the fray.

"You've done well for yourself, girl. Hard to find a guy with brains and brawn!"

"Hank's really good at his job," Olivia agreed, dropping some of her hauteur.

"Sales is not for everyone," Jenny prompted. "He must like talking to people."

"Oh yes," Olivia said proudly. "He's one of the most sought after reps at his company."

She named a big drug company known for producing a broad range of medicines.

"Hank's a top pharmaceutical salesman, then," Jenny spoke. "He must make a lot of money."

"I don't care about that," Olivia rolled her eyes. "I've got my own fortune."

She took a big sip of her drink and twisted her mouth.

"All the ice has melted."

Jenny offered to get her fresh drinks.

"Never mind," Olivia cribbed. "I don't want to keep Hank waiting."

Heather high fived Jenny as soon as Olivia stepped out of the café.

"That was brilliant."

Jenny pulled her into the kitchen.

"Didn't I say this guy was important?" she nudged Heather. "He works for a drug company, Heather. Just think about it."

"You mean he could have poisoned Bella?"

"I am not going that far," Jenny said cautiously. "At least not yet."

"But he had access to drugs," Heather summed up.

"We need to find out more about him," Jenny said, pressing her lips together.

Heather watched as Jenny mixed some muffin batter for a fresh batch.

"I'll tell you what I need," she said, adding cheese to the batter. "I need a vacation."

"Why don't you go on a solo trip somewhere?" Jenny suggested. "I think you will enjoy it."

Heather shook her head.

"We should all go. I'm going to do some research on this."

"You do that," Jenny nodded. "It has to be child friendly though. I won't go anywhere without Emily."

Betty Sue and Molly swept in one after the other and went out to the deck.

"I'm craving something salty," Betty Sue announced, her hands busy knitting a pair of pink socks.

"I have just the thing," Jenny promised her, placing a batch of hot tomato, cheese and ham muffins before her.

Star was quiet as she nibbled on a muffin. Betty Sue tapped the table with her knuckles.

"Is Barb bothering you again? I thought you reached an agreement about that film festival."

"I'm not worried about Barb," Star said grumpily.

Molly pulled her head out of her book and squealed suddenly.

"You never told us about your date. So did Jimmy propose?"

Star shook her head.

"He was very kind. He said he wasn't about to do anything against my wishes. He just wanted to show me a good time."

"That's what you wanted, isn't it?" Betty Sue thundered.

"I don't know," Star said uncertainly. "I guess a part of me wanted some kind of gesture."

"You are being irrational," Jenny told her aunt. "All this time, you were fussing because you didn't want Jimmy to speed things up. Now you're mad because he did exactly what you wanted?"

"It's all your fault," Star accused. "You raised my hopes."

"Stop being an idiot," Betty Sue snapped. "Don't

tempt fate. You've got a good thing going here. Quit whining and enjoy it while you can."

Star's eyes welled up with tears.

Jenny stroked her back and urged her to cheer up.

"I do love him, you know. I hope he knows that."

"You are not very open about it, Star," Jenny winced. "You keep the poor man on a short leash."

"Is that what you think?" Star asked, aghast.

She looked at the Magnolias one by one. They nodded reluctantly.

"What am I going to do?" Star wailed. "I have been a fool."

"It's not too late," Jenny soothed. "Just show him you care about him. Do something he likes, Star."

Heather had pulled something up on her phone.

"Here are ten ideas to make your man feel special," she said, thrusting the phone in Star's face.

"I don't need that," Star said, finally cracking a smile. "I know what I'm going to do."

"Hey, look," Heather whispered, trying to get Jenny's attention. "Looks like Olivia's coming in for a second round."

Jenny was staring at the blonde, blue eyed man who was coming up the steps with Olivia. His broken nose made him look rugged but more attractive.

"More lemonade?" Jenny asked Olivia.

Betty Sue was staring at Hank.

"Are you Bill Murphy's son?" she asked, pointing a finger at him. "You look just like he did when he was younger."

Hank nodded.

"Is your family back in town?" she asked. "Why wasn't I told?"

Betty Sue was the reigning queen of Pelican Cove. Most of the old families regularly visited her to pay their respects. Many didn't make life altering decisions without getting her blessing.

"The family lives in the city now," Hank explained. "I'm here on business."

Betty Sue gave him a quelling look and went back to her knitting.

"Hank's a Murphy?" Heather cried as soon as Olivia had left with him.

"He said so, didn't he?" Betty Sue muttered.

"Who are these Murphys?" Jenny asked curiously.

Betty Sue exhaled heavily.

"This was before your time, Jenny. The Murphy family came off the Isabella."

"Just like the Worthingtons?" Jenny prompted.

"Those two families were very close. They started the button factory together and built their fortunes. Things fell apart ten years ago."

"What happened?" Jenny asked, waiting with bated breath.

"Max and Billie had a falling out. Max accused Billie of pilfering money. He blamed Max instead. Rumor has it, they threatened to kill each other. Within a week, the Murphys shut up their house and moved to the city. They were never seen here again."

"So the Murphys and Worthingtons hate each other ..." Jenny said softly.

Betty Sue nodded vigorously.

"Their feud made headlines ten years ago."

"What's Hank doing with Olivia then?" Jenny

wondered. "It makes no sense."

"Young people these days …" Betty Sue clucked. "They have no sense of loyalty."

"Wait a minute," Heather interrupted. "Hank's father had a feud with Max, right? What if Hank is using Olivia to get to him?"

"You think that boy is here for revenge?"

Jenny felt a shiver run through her body.

"Max may be rich and powerful but he had a weakness."

"Bella!" Heather agreed with a nod. "Max's daughter was his Achilles heel."

"What if Hank decided to strike where it would hurt most?" Jenny asked, wide eyed.

"That's absurd!" Betty Sue cried. "The Murphys were a good family."

"We don't really know Hank, Grandma," Heather said. "And we can't overlook he was at Bella's party."

"That's right," Jenny said with a frown. "He was in town the night Bella died."

Chapter 18

Jenny and Heather sat in the living room of the Worthington mansion, waiting for Olivia. Jenny had decided to confront her as soon as possible.

Max Worthington strode in, his hair still damp from the shower. His suit jacket was missing and so was his tie. He glanced at his watch irritably and scowled at Jenny.

"It's barely 7 AM. What are you doing here so early, Miss King?"

"We are here to meet Olivia," Heather informed him.

"My niece? What's she got to do with you?"

Olivia ambled in before Jenny could respond. She was wearing pajamas with little puppies on them. Her hair was in disarray and she let out a big yawn as she stared at Jenny through bleary eyes.

"What are you doing here?" she asked Jenny.

Max glared at Olivia, clucking with disapproval at her appearance.

"Forget about them for a minute. Why aren't you

dressed yet? We have a 7:30 AM conference call with our associates in China."

Olivia's hand flew to her mouth.

"Is that today?" she asked. "I didn't realize."

"Clearly, you have overslept," her uncle thundered. "What have I told you about the early bird?"

"I'm sorry," she muttered. "I got in late last night."

"Having too much fun?" Heather nagged.

Max was looking furious.

"Bella had a curfew of 10 PM on weeknights. I think you should follow the same, Olivia."

"I'm too old for curfews, Uncle," Olivia said sweetly.

"You will follow the rules of this house as long as you are living here," Max growled.

Olivia turned red and pushed out her lower lip.

"Are you also going to control who I date?" she fumed.

"I think the ship has already sailed on that one," Jenny said, jumping into the conversation.

"Don't you meddle in our family matter," Max warned.

"State your business and leave at once."

"I'm coming to it," Jenny said calmly. "Do you know who your niece is going around with?"

"No, but I am going to find out," Max replied, giving Olivia a meaningful look.

"Hank Murphy," Heather supplied. "Does the name ring a bell?"

"Murphy?" Max sputtered. "Not Bill Murphy's son?"

"The very same," Jenny said, folding her hands.

Max turned red as a tomato. A vein in his forehead threatened to pop as he glowered at Olivia.

"What are you doing with the Murphy boy? Are you out of your mind?"

Olivia was looking bewildered. She flopped down in a chair and looked uncomprehendingly at her uncle.

"The Murphys almost destroyed our family," Max screeched. "They were going to put your father in jail."

"What's Hank got to do with any of that?" Olivia cried.

"I forbid you to see this boy," Max bellowed. "Absolutely forbid it."

"You can't do that," Olivia sulked. "We love each other."

Jenny cleared her throat.

"Are you sure about that?"

Max paced the room with his hands behind his back, growing angrier by the minute.

"This is our private matter. Why are you here anyway?"

"I think Hank came here with a purpose," Jenny told him. "He wanted to get close to Bella."

Max's eyebrows shot up and his eyes grew wide in disbelief.

"You think he hurt my baby?"

"It's too soon to say anything definite," Jenny admitted. "But it's a possibility."

"I think it's a ridiculous idea," Olivia dismissed.

"Where did you meet Hank?" Heather questioned. "Why did he come to Pelican Cove, huh?"

"Hank's a sales rep for a pharmaceutical company," Olivia told them. "He's on the road a lot. He has to meet doctors and visit pharmacies all the time."

"If he's lying, we'll find out soon enough," Jenny said.

"Are you done spreading your venom?" Olivia snapped.

Max had calmed down a bit.

"Go get ready, Olivia," he ordered. He turned toward Jenny. "Do the police know about this boy?"

"Not from me," Jenny replied. "I may be wrong about him, Mr. Worthington."

Max clasped his hands and stared in the distance.

"There is a lot of bad blood between the Murphys and the Worthingtons. I am sure the boy came here with a nefarious purpose. The question is, how far did he go?"

Jenny promised Max she would get to the bottom of it.

"Where to now?" Heather asked when they piled into Jenny's car.

"Let's resolve this," Jenny said. "Why don't we go and see old Dr. Smith? If Hank's really here to visit doctors, he must have gone to his clinic."

The doctor assured them he had never come across Hank. Jenny and Heather went back to the Boardwalk Café, trying to guess what Hank was really up to.

The Magnolias were sitting out on the deck, waiting for

them to get back. The sun was out after two days of rain. Seagulls rode the waves, calling to each other with their distinctive cries. Jenny tried to gather her thoughts as she watched a couple walk on the beach, hand in hand. It triggered a memory she would rather forget.

Heather's shrill voice penetrated the fog in her brain.

"I'm starving! We had to miss breakfast."

Star pointed toward a plate of muffins on the table and offered to make a pimento cheese sandwich.

"Thanks," Heather smiled. "But these are fine for now. Wait till you hear what we found out."

Jenny quickly brought them up to speed.

"You don't think the Murphy boy comes to town just to woo this girl?" Betty Sue asked.

"It's hard to say," Jenny replied. "According to Olivia, he is here to sell his products to the doctors. But there's only one doctor in town and he doesn't know Hank."

"He could be visiting the neighboring towns," Star pointed out. "He might be using Pelican Cove as a base to travel up and down the Shore."

Molly looked up from her book.

"I forgot to tell you. I saw Hank at the pharmacy last week. He was coming out of that little room they have in the back."

"That's where they keep the special drugs," Star said. "What was he doing in there?"

Molly shrugged and went back to her book.

"What if he's dealing drugs on the side?" Heather asked, chewing with her mouth open.

Betty Sue elbowed her and told her off for talking with a mouthful of food.

"That's not very farfetched," Jenny reasoned. "If he works for a drug company, he must have access to them."

"Don't these people have a lot of samples?" Molly asked. "Just saying."

"The Murphys were a good family," Betty Sue protested. "I don't think this boy could stoop to murder."

"He might, if he had a strong enough motive," Jenny said. "I need to look at Calvin's autopsy report again. I want to see if he was poisoned too."

Jenny went inside and called Jason.

"Can you pull in a favor?" she cajoled. "I really want to see what's in Calvin's report."

Jason turned up for lunch a couple of hours later, holding a file in his hand.

"Is that it?" Jenny asked eagerly.

"Don't you have a hug for your loving husband?" Jason asked, opening his arms wide.

Jenny snuggled into him and planted a quick kiss on his forehead. Then she grabbed the file and flipped through it impatiently.

"That's it," she said, jabbing her finger at a spot. "How did I miss this?"

"What is it, Jenny?" Jason asked, peering over her shoulder.

"They found a common painkiller in his body, an opioid."

"Opium overdoses can be fatal, Jenny."

Jenny shook her head.

"It says here the amount of opium wasn't enough to kill him."

"Maybe they used just enough to put him to sleep,"

Jason suggested.

"Either that, or Calvin was an addict."

"You think someone's dealing drugs to high school kids?" Jason wondered. "I didn't realize such things happened in Pelican Cove."

"I have a very good idea who might have done this," Jenny said grimly, picking up her car keys to head out.

Jason convinced her to stay and have a spot of lunch with him.

"Be careful, Jenny," he warned as he sipped his chicken soup. "Emily and I need you to be safe."

Jenny assured him she wouldn't take any unnecessary risks.

She packed a basket with food and set off to meet Francine, Calvin's neighbor.

Jenny parked her car on the deserted street and looked around. Not a single person was in sight. Jenny wondered if the neighborhood was more lively on the weekends.

Francine sat on the porch with a book in her hands. Her face lit up when she saw Jenny.

"Hello," Jenny greeted her. "Remember me?"

"Of course I remember you, Jenny," Francine chuckled. "My mind's not gone yet."

Jenny rushed to apologize.

"Relax," Francine said. "Take a load off."

Jenny placed the basket of food on the rickety table.

"I brought you some stuff."

Francine rifled through the basket eagerly. She opened the container of soup and sniffed appreciatively.

"My niece couldn't make it this morning," she told Jenny. "I haven't had lunch. Could you heat some of this soup for me please?"

Jenny couldn't say no. She went in and ladled some soup into a bowl. It went into the microwave while Jenny put the pimento cheese sandwich she had brought on a plate. She spotted a bag of chips on the counter and poured some next to the sandwich. She took the tray of food out to Francine.

Francine took a sip of soup and gave her a thumbs up.

"Homemade soup is a treat. Did you make this yourself?"

Jenny nodded and promised to bring Francine to the Boardwalk Café sometime.

"What brings you here today?" Francine asked after she had put away a fair amount of the food.

"I found some stuff about Calvin," Jenny told her. "Not all good, I'm afraid."

"Calvin was a troubled kid," Francine said. "But he wouldn't hurt anyone."

"He was on drugs," Jenny told her. "Opiates."

Francine didn't look surprised.

"I caught him sneaking a bottle of my pain pills once. I tried to talk to his parents. But they wouldn't believe me."

"When did this happen?"

"A few months ago," Francine said, squinting her eyes. "Hard to say how he picked up the habit."

"I think I might know who supplied him with drugs," Jenny replied.

She shuffled through the pictures on her phone and pulled up a photo of Hank Murphy.

"Do you recognize him?" she asked Francine.

Francine bobbed her head vigorously.

"I have seen that boy more than once. He came to visit

Calvin."

"Thanks. That's very helpful."

"He doesn't look like a drug dealer," Francine said. "He looks like a nice boy from a good family."

"Appearances can be deceptive," Jenny muttered as she said goodbye to Francine.

"Thanks for the food," Francine called out after her.

Jenny drove around, trying to figure out her next steps. She wanted to confront Hank Murphy right away. Then she remembered Jason's warning. She pulled up on the shoulder and called Heather. The two friends agreed to meet at the Rusty Anchor.

Jenny wondered if she was close to finding out what happened to Bella. She parked her car outside the pub and went in, eager to share her latest findings with Heather. She was so engrossed in her thoughts she barely realized where she was going until she walked into a man standing at the bar.

A pair of hands grabbed her arms in a vice like grip. Jenny looked up to see Hank Murphy's icy blue eyes flashing fire at her.

Was she staring into the eyes of a killer?

Chapter 19

Jenny and Heather sat at their usual table at the Rusty Anchor. Jenny sipped her glass of wine while she watched Olivia and Hank canoodling at the bar.

"What are you waiting for?" Heather asked, getting restless. "Let's talk to him right now. Shall I call him over?"

Jenny raised a hand and caught the bartender's attention. She pointed at Olivia. Olivia whirled around and gave her a smoldering look. She marched to their table, dragging Hank behind her.

"Haven't you done enough damage for one day?" she scowled. "My uncle's threatening to fire me if I continue meeting Hank."

"Sit down," Jenny ordered. "Both of you."

She placed her hands on the table and trained her eyes on Hank.

"We know what you are up to, Hank. Dealing drugs to school kids. Aren't you ashamed of yourself?"

Hank folded his arms and stared back at Jenny, refusing to back down.

"You don't have any proof."

"I can get proof if I want to," Jenny shot back. "So you don't deny it?"

"What's the use?"

Olivia was looking stricken.

"What is she saying, Hank?"

"Tell her," Heather nodded. "Tell her you were just using her all this time."

Hank gritted his teeth.

"I wanted to teach them a lesson. The Worthingtons put my family through hell. I was just a twelve year old kid. We had to pack up and leave town overnight."

"What does that have to do with me?" Olivia cried.

"You are a Worthington, aren't you?" Hank asked bitterly. "You are one of them."

"So you don't love me?"

Jenny felt sorry for Olivia. Hank seemed to have no such regrets. He gave a shrug and looked away.

"Why me?" Olivia asked. "Why punish me for something my uncle did?"

Hank rolled his eyes.

"Don't you get it? You were just a means to an end. Bella was the one I was really after."

"That's why you convinced me to go to that party," Olivia said in a hushed voice. "I didn't really want to go."

"You got it, babe," Hank leered. "I had plans for Bella. But then you got us thrown out."

"You had enough time to poison Bella though," Jenny said.

"Hardly," Hank sighed.

"We know you were supplying opium to Calvin, Hank. You were seen at his house multiple times. Did you use the same thing with Bella?"

"I'm telling you I never got close enough," Hank insisted. "I had an elaborate plan. I mixed up a few samples I had and made a special cocktail for Bella. I was going to slip it into her drink."

"You wanted to finish her on the spot?" Heather asked.

Hank shook his head.

"It wasn't going to be lethal. I was there to keep an eye

on her. I just wanted her to lose control and do something crazy. I know a guy who works at a tabloid."

"You wanted to defame her," Jenny deduced.

"Not just her," Hank said viciously. "Her entire family. I wanted them to know how it feels to be discredited before all your friends."

"But you didn't give her this drug cocktail?" Jenny pressed.

"Unfortunately not," Hank said, planting a fist on the table. "It was all for nothing."

Olivia collapsed into a chair and burst into tears.

"Beat it," Heather told Hank.

Jenny offered a tissue to Olivia and poured her a glass of water. She rubbed the poor girl's back, feeling sorry for her.

"I've been such a fool," Olivia sobbed through her tears. "I fell for his false charm."

"You are not to blame here," Jenny soothed. "He purposely set out to dupe you."

"He is a handsome devil," Heather said. "Any young girl would have fallen for his looks."

"You are too kind," Olivia said, wiping her tears. "But if Hank didn't poison Bella, who did?"

"At least Hank was out to get revenge," Jenny said. "Why would anyone else want to hurt Bella? She was such a sweet kid."

"She was a bit too free with her favors," Olivia spoke up.

"You mean she was cheating on Jake?" Heather asked.

"That's not what I mean," Olivia said, shaking her head. "I mean people took advantage of her. They stuck to her like leeches."

"You have said that before," Heather told her. "More than once."

"It's true!" Olivia exclaimed. "Take Sam for instance. He barely has two pennies to rub together. He mooched all his meals off Bella. Have you seen that guy eat? And that's not all. Bella even let him use her shower."

Jenny thought of the dilapidated trailer Sam lived in.

"Maybe she was just helping him out," she said meekly.

"You have to draw the line somewhere," Olivia said in protest. "Bella didn't have any boundaries. And her so called friends took full advantage of that."

"Sam's really beaten up about Bella. So is Ashley. They might have sponged stuff off her but they loved her."

"Ashley's just a copycat," Olivia burst out. "She was jealous of every little thing Bella had. But of course she couldn't afford the nice stuff."

Jenny thought about the designer labels Bella had worn. Then she remembered how Ashley always looked like a cheaper version of Bella.

"She did try to look like Bella, I guess," she admitted.

"Ashley wore cheap knockoffs," Olivia nodded. "You know what she did at Bella's engagement party?"

Heather and Jenny shook their heads, waiting for her to go on.

"She wore the same dress as Bella, only hers came from a supermarket hanger."

"Bella was okay with that?" Heather asked.

"Not this time," Olivia said smugly. "Bella could be a pushover but she held her ground this time. They had a big fight."

"Why did no one mention this before?" Jenny asked.

"This was at home," Olivia explained. "I heard them arguing in Bella's room. That's how I found out about the party."

"Tell us more," Jenny prompted. "Who stepped down?"

"Neither of them was ready to budge," Olivia relayed. "Bella offered her entire wardrobe to Ashley and told her to choose any dress she wanted. But Ashley wouldn't listen."

"That doesn't sound like Ashley," Jenny said. "She pretty much sang Bella's tune all the time."

"Not that day. The last I saw, they were pulling each other's hair out."

"They must have made up though," Heather pointed out. "Otherwise Ashley wouldn't have been at the party."

"You don't think Ashley was still holding a grudge?" Olivia asked slyly.

"Are you suggesting Ashley would hurt Bella over a dress?" Jenny was incredulous. "They were best friends."

"You never really know, do you?" Olivia said bitterly. "Look at Hank and me. I thought we were in love."

"Bella and Ashley have been friends since kindergarten," Heather argued. "You just met Hank.

It's not the same."

"If you say so." Olivia gave a shrug.

Jenny and Heather let Olivia regale them with several anecdotes of people exploiting Bella's generosity. Jenny decided it was a case of sour grapes.

Heather reminded Jenny they needed to get going. The Magnolias were having a spa night at Seaview, Jenny's home. They bid goodbye to Olivia and headed out.

"Did you believe all that rot she was spouting?" Heather asked as soon as they got into the car.

"I was barely listening," Jenny admitted. "I was thinking of Emily."

Jenny rushed up the stairs to the nursery as soon as she got home. Emily was sleeping peacefully in her crib.

"I put her down some time ago," the nanny told her.

They talked about the highlights of Emily's day. Jenny planted a soft kiss on the baby's forehead and freshened up in her room before meeting her friends.

Heather was enjoying a plate of Star's Quattro Formaggi lasagna. Jenny fixed a plate for herself and joined the ladies in the living room.

"You look all done in," Molly said, looking up from

painting her nails. "What took you so long?"

Heather twisted her mouth in disapproval.

"Olivia just went on and on with her complaints."

"She's singing a different tune, isn't she?" Jenny asked between bites.

"I say she's trying to shift focus away from herself," Heather guessed. "We can't forget she's still a suspect."

"But I thought she's not going to inherit," Molly said.

"She's not," Jenny agreed. "But she didn't know that until after Bella died."

"So you haven't narrowed down your list at all?" Betty Sue inquired.

"Ashley was on the spot but she almost died herself," Jenny said. "I think we can rule her out."

"What about that fight they had just before the party?" Heather reminded her. "I think Ashley could still have done it. Her plan backfired and she escaped by a narrow margin."

"What about Max?" Betty Sue asked. "Did he put his family's honor above his daughter?"

"Max might be a narcissist, but he wouldn't hurt his

child," Jenny protested. "You haven't seen how cut up he is about Bella's death."

"Hank Murphy had intent but he never got around to doing his bad deed," Heather added. "Are we going to believe him, Jenny?"

"What about Jake?" Molly asked. "That lazy bum?"

"He's too languid to lift a finger," Heather laughed. "I doubt he got off his back long enough to plan such an elaborate crime."

"Jokes apart," Jenny said. "Jake doesn't have a motive. He was planning to elope with Bella. In a way, he was marrying a bag of money. And they were in love."

"What if Jake still had feelings for Ashley?" Heather asked.

"He would just have broken up with Bella," Jenny argued. "And I think you got that wrong. Ashley is the one who was sweet on Jake."

"That brings us back to Ashley," Heather shot back. "Maybe Ashley couldn't bear to see Jake and Bella get engaged. So she decided to get Bella out of the way."

"Where does Sam fit into all this?" Molly asked.

Jenny scraped the last bite of lasagna from her plate and got up to get a second helping.

"Bella was Sam's guardian angel," she said over her shoulder as she went into the kitchen. "Sam's life has gone downhill in the past few weeks."

"Sam has no motive," Heather dismissed.

"I think we are forgetting one more person," Jenny said, settling into her spot on the couch. "Calvin?"

"But Calvin's dead!" Heather exclaimed. "And the police already quashed the suicide theory."

"I think our original theory has some merit," Jenny mused. "Calvin went after the girls, didn't he? He could have caused that accident."

"Who do you think killed Calvin then?" Heather's expression was skeptical at best.

"We know Calvin was into drugs," Jenny reminded her. "Maybe he owed money to someone, or got into a gang."

Heather's eyebrows shot up in disbelief.

"Calvin Butler? That poor nerd? No way Calvin was part of a gang."

"That's enough, you two," Betty Sue stepped in. "Take a break from all this."

"It's not making much sense anyway," Heather

grumbled.

Star had been quiet all this time.

"Whoever it was, I think it was someone close to Bella. Someone she trusted completely. That's the only way anyone could drug her."

"And this person had to be on the spot," Heather stressed.

"We don't know how fast acting the drug was," Jenny argued. "What if she drank something before going to the party? Max could have handed it to her. Or Olivia. Or that butler."

"You need to unwind now, Jenny," Molly said calmly. "Put on the lavender face mask I made and let go."

Jenny nodded without protest and spoke under her breath. "Live to fight another day."

Chapter 20

Another bright and sunny day dawned in Pelican Cove. The Boardwalk Café was almost full with a fresh lot of tourists. Jenny had a smile on her face as she made crab omelets for breakfast. Spa night with her friends had worked wonders for her.

Star had come in early to help. She was going on a lunch date with Jimmy later. Jenny took advantage of a temporary lull and fixed some eggs and bacon for herself. She took it out to the deck. For once, Jenny's mind was calm as she gazed at the ocean, thinking about her day. She was planning to take Emily to the zoo after she was done at the café.

Jenny waved at some regular walkers and observed the different bathing suits on display. She thought of her own worn out one-piece and decided to treat herself to a new one. A tanned, muscular youth reposed in a faded camp chair, arms above his head. He caught Jenny's eye and raised a hand in greeting. Jenny waved back.

She went in and started fixing a jumbo breakfast sandwich worthy of a teenager. She put the crab omelet between toasted croissant buns, added bacon, cheese, fried potatoes and gravy. She purposely left out the tomatoes. She put the sandwich in a paper bag, filled a large cup with coffee and went out to the beach.

"Is that for me?" Jake asked in surprise when Jenny handed it all over.

"Something new on the café menu," Jenny explained. "I'm always looking for tasters."

"Don't mind if I do," Jake beamed, taking a healthy bite of the sandwich.

"You're out awfully early," Jenny said, sitting cross legged on the beach.

"It's not like I have anywhere else to be," Jake said seriously. "I already have my GED. I'm a free bird until college starts in fall."

"I usually take on extra help in the summer," Jenny told him. "Let me know if you are interested."

Jake promised to think about it.

"Are you just here to shoot the breeze?" he asked. "Or did you have something on your mind."

"It's about Bella," Jenny admitted. "Do you mind talking about her?"

Jake slammed a pair of dark shades on his face.

"That's about all I can do now," he sighed. "What do you want to know?"

"Nothing particular," Jenny said. "Just tell me about her. I might learn something I missed earlier."

Jake told her how Bella had been popular with everyone at school. She was head cheerleader and student council president. She had been homecoming queen and was the top choice for prom queen.

"How did you two get together?" Jenny asked curiously. "Was it while you were still going to school?"

Jake looked sheepish. He had formally met Bella when he had been dating Ashley. She had wanted to bring the two of them together. He was drawn to her instantly. Jenny wondered who had initiated the breakup with Ashley.

"I think it was love at first sight," Jake told her. "I broke up with Ashley right after that."

"How did she take it?"

"She wasn't happy, of course." Jake gave a shrug. "She didn't have a choice."

"Did you start dating Bella right away?"

Jake told her how Bella had refused to meet him for

several days after that.

"She always felt guilty, you know," he explained. "She thought she was cheating on her friend."

"But you weren't seeing them both at the same time?"

"Of course not!" Jake sat up indignantly. "What kind of guy do you think I am?"

"Tell me more," Jenny urged. "Were you intimidated by her wealth?"

"Bella liked to show off," Jake agreed. "But she was so generous with her money, you couldn't really stay mad at her."

"I know something about that," Jenny admitted. "Bella hired a limo for our trip to the mountains. Said it was her treat."

"That was chump change for her," Jake said, warming up to his theme. "She poured boatloads of money into lost causes. Take that weight loss supplement of Sam's, for instance."

"Tell me more."

"Sam had this brilliant idea about developing a wonder drug from some herbs. He needed an investor. Guess who jumped in with both feet?"

"I thought Sam was on some secret diet," Jenny supplied. "He never mentioned a drug."

"Bella was all gung-ho about it. Gave him a big chunk of money to develop a sample. And she was ready to give him more. Took me all I got to talk her out of it."

Jenny chatted with Jake some more. Then she went back inside to prep for lunch. Jenny mixed strawberry chicken salad and frosted a six layer chocolate cake. She called Jason and asked him over for lunch.

By the time Jenny could join her husband out on the deck, he had already finished his sandwich. He was waiting with a fork in his hand, admiring the big slice of chocolate cake before him.

"Are you still going to the city?" Jenny asked him.

Jason nodded as he took a bite. He was going to be late getting back home.

"Any update on Ashley?" Jenny asked him.

"She admits she was driving under the influence. The police are definitely going to charge her."

"What about those drugs they found in Bella?" Jenny asked. "Can't you find out more about them?"

"I'm working on it." Jason stood up and gave Jenny a quick hug. "Off I go. Don't wait up."

Jenny was clearing the table when she heard someone wheezing. Sam was climbing up the café steps, covered in sweat.

"Hey Sam!" she greeted him. "How are you?"

Sam collapsed in a chair and pulled a wad of paper napkins out of the dispenser. He wiped his face and neck and exhaled noisily.

"You don't look too good." Jenny looked at him with concern.

"I'm fine," Sam assured her. "Sweating is a perfectly natural function of the body. I am getting rid of all those nasty toxins."

"You've been holding out on me," Jenny said, her hands on her hips. "I know you've found some miracle cure for weight loss."

Sam looked around furtively. There was no one else on the deck.

"Nothing's definite yet. I'm still working on it."

"Don't keep it to yourself," Jenny coaxed. "I could stand to lose a few pounds myself."

"I can't talk about it here," Sam whispered. "Why don't you come out to my trailer later today?"

Jenny agreed to meet him there. Sam devoured a few sandwiches and two slices of cake before he left.

Jenny worked through the lunch crowd and stared at the clock in dismay. She would have to hurry if she wanted to still visit Sam and keep her date with Emily.

Sam sat on a box outside his trailer, waiting for Jenny. He had changed into a clean shirt. An easel had been set up and a plate of brownies reposed on the trestle table.

"I have made a small presentation," Sam declared proudly, pointing at the easel.

"That sounds formal," Jenny said, impressed.

"It was Bella's idea," Sam said. "But I never got a chance to show it to her."

"Bella knew about all this?" Jenny asked cagily.

"Bella was my angel. She supported me in every way possible."

Sam's face crumpled and his eyes filled up.

"Bella would want you to go on," Jenny reminded him. "I'm sure she was proud of you."

Sam blinked away his tears and gave a watery smile. He asked Jenny to try the brownies.

"I baked them especially for you."

Jenny took a bite and prompted Sam to begin. Sam walked her through his business plan, showing her charts and diagrams until her head started to reel.

"You've done a good job, Sam," she lauded. "Very professional."

Sam named a big amount. He needed it to produce a sample batch of his product.

"I'm sorry to interrupt," Jenny said, finally glancing at her watch. "But I need to leave. I have to take my daughter somewhere."

Jenny rushed home, realizing she was already running late. Emily was waiting on the porch with the nanny. She dissolved into smiles when she saw Jenny and held up her arms.

Jenny scooped Emily up and planted a bunch of kisses on her face.

"Are we all set to leave?"

The nanny pointed at a large bag bursting with toys and food and nodded. Five minutes later, they were off. Jenny played some nursery rhymes in the car and sang along with them. Emily clapped her hands and joined in.

Jenny was near the edge of town, about to take the bridge off the island when the first cramp hit her. Her stomach seemed to convulse and she puked her guts out in the car before she could pull over. Jenny stumbled out of the car and proceeded to be sick for the next ten minutes. Her pain was so intense she could barely stand.

"We need to get you to the hospital," the nanny said grimly. "I'm calling an ambulance right now."

Jenny convinced the nanny to drive them to the emergency room.

Jason rushed into Jenny's room three hours later, his eyes clouded with worry.

"How are you, Jenny?" he asked, rushing to her side. "How did this happen?"

"The doctor thinks she was drugged," Star said grimly. "They pumped her stomach just in time."

Betty Sue and Heather nodded in agreement. Star was still listed as Jenny's emergency contact so she had been called when Jenny checked in. The Magnolias had rushed to the hospital as soon as they could. Star sent the nanny home with the baby.

"You mean someone did this on purpose?" Jason asked, aghast.

He clasped Jenny's hand and gaped at her, unable to hide his desperation.

"I'm sorry, Jason," Jenny mumbled weakly. "I don't know how ..."

"It's clear as crystal, Jenny," Heather said. "You managed to spook someone. You are getting close."

Jason simmered with barely controlled anger.

"Who did this, Jenny? Whose toes have you trampled on now?"

Chapter 21

Heather plumped up the pillows on Jenny's bed and asked her if she was comfortable.

"I'm fine! Stop fussing over me."

"Have you made a list of everything you ate yesterday?" Heather reminded her.

"I don't need to. Must have been some bad shrimp."

Heather rolled her eyes.

"We are not dealing with bad seafood here, Jenny. The doctors are sure there was something in your food."

"I cooked it all myself," Jenny muttered. "Do you think I poisoned my food and then forgot about it?"

"This is not funny!"

Jason swept into the room, holding his phone aloft. Jenny took one look at his face and tried to sit up.

"What is it?" she asked in alarm.

"Good news for my client," Jason crowed, pumping his fist in the air. "They have nothing against Ashley now."

Jenny waited for her husband to settle down and explain what had happened.

"I got a final copy of Bella's autopsy report. It says all her injuries happened post mortem."

"What does that mean?"

"Bella was already dead when Ashley crashed the car."

"How could this be?" Jenny cried.

"The poison killed her, Jenny," Jason elaborated. "The only person hurt in that accident was Ashley."

"So the police might charge her with drunk driving but they can't hold her responsible for Bella's death," Jenny summed up.

"Ashley's blood alcohol content was marginal. I might be able to get her off with a warning."

"So we are looking for someone who had knowledge of drugs," Heather spoke up. "Hank Murphy!"

"I don't think it was a conventional poison. The report mentions some plant residue."

"Like deadly mushrooms?" Heather asked.

"Could be," Jason said. "Do you know anyone who works with herbs or plants?"

Jenny sat up with a jerk.

"Sam! He's working on a plant based weight loss supplement."

"Sam?" Heather chuckled. "He was crazy about Bella. Why would he poison her?"

"I don't know what his motive was, but we need to call the police right away."

Jenny told them about her meeting with Sam the previous day.

"Why haven't you mentioned these brownies before?" Jason burst out.

"I forgot," Jenny dismissed. "That's not important right now. We need to catch him before he escapes."

Jason placed a call to the police and handed over the phone to Jenny. She gave a concise report of why she suspected Sam.

"They said they will look into it," Jenny griped as she hung up the phone.

Jason warned Jenny to stay in bed and left for work.

"Why are you treating me like an invalid?" Jenny railed at Heather. "I'm perfectly fine now."

"You are severely dehydrated," Heather reminded her. "You need to rest for a couple of days."

She picked up an empty flask from Jenny's bedside table.

"I'm going to get you more water. Or do you prefer some herbal tea?"

"Can you check on Emily for me please?" Jenny asked.

Heather came back with a tray loaded with hibiscus tea, followed by the nanny and Emily. The baby was clutching a doll in one hand and sucking her thumb. Jenny played with her for some time until the nanny took her away for a snack.

Jason called with an update.

"What's going on?" Heather asked eagerly, looking up from her phone.

"They raided his trailer. It seems he had set up a makeshift laboratory in that trailer next to his. They found a lot of plants there. I don't think the police are familiar with what every plant does. They might have to bring in some expert."

"What about Sam?" Heather asked impatiently. "Did they find him there or what?"

"Sam had already flown the coop."

Heather swore under her breath.

"Don't worry," Jenny said, holding up her hand. "They got him. He was halfway across the bridge when they caught him and brought him in. He is being questioned as we speak."

"At least you are safe for now," Heather sighed.

Heather urged Jenny to take a nap. Jenny protested strongly but finally drifted off to sleep. She woke up just before the Magnolias arrived around 4 PM. Ignoring Heather's protests, she went down to the living room to meet everyone.

Star had kept the café going with some help from Molly.

Betty Sue's jaw dropped when Jenny told them about Sam.

"You never suspected him, did you?" she asked Jenny.

"Not really," Jenny admitted. "Hank was top on my list after we found out he had access to drugs. So was Olivia. I eliminated Ashley a while ago and I wasn't sure about Calvin. But I never thought Sam might be involved."

"What about that boyfriend of hers?" Molly asked.

"Jake? I wasn't crazy about him either." Jenny shook

her head. "He seemed cocky."

"Do you think Sam might have had an accomplice?" Heather wondered.

"I don't know," Jenny sighed. "But I guess we'll find out soon enough."

Star reminisced about their trip to the mountains. Everyone had fond memories of Bella.

"Poor girl," Betty Sue clucked. "She was just surrounded by sinners."

"Everyone close to her had an axe to grind," Jenny agreed. "Even her father."

They moved to the kitchen after some time and Star started dinner. She was making a casserole big enough to feed everyone. No one was budging until they had more news.

Jason arrived in a flurry and sat down heavily at the kitchen table. All pairs of eyes looked at him expectantly.

"He did it. Sam confessed."

Everyone exhaled noisily. Star placed a bowl of trail mix before Jason and poured him a glass of tea.

"Go on," Jenny prompted. "We've been twiddling our

thumbs all day, waiting for an update."

"I am just coming from the police station," Jason told them, sipping his tea gratefully. "They weren't very forthcoming but I managed to squeeze the story out of them."

"Did he drug those brownies he gave Jenny?" Heather asked impatiently.

"Hold your horses, Heather. Let him start from the top."

"Sam had some wild idea about producing a miracle drug," Jason started. "It was entirely plant based and supposed to have no side effects."

"Who would have guessed Sam had the brains?" Heather interrupted. "They said he had been held back. He was older than Bella and Ashley."

"I don't think that had anything to do with his intellect," Jason said. "Sam was shuffled from one foster home to another. He might even have been in some kind of juvenile detention. He must have missed school because of that."

"Plant based medicine is a vast field," Star said. "Where did he learn about that?"

"One of his foster parents was an herbalist. He picked up some knowledge from her, it seems."

"Get back to the main story," Jenny prompted. "So he was going to produce this miracle drug. What happened after that?"

"Bella supported him," Jason explained. "She gave him a chunk of money to start working on a prototype but he needed much more."

"Did she say no?" Heather asked. "Did they have a falling out?"

"Jake arrived on the scene. He saw Bella doling out money to anyone who asked for it. He felt they were taking advantage of her."

"I guess they were," Jenny nodded, remembering her conversation with Jake.

"He convinced her to be more discerning. Bella became tight fisted."

"She cut off Sam's funding?"

"She didn't," Jason sighed. "At least she hadn't until she was alive. But Sam expected her to, especially when he learned about Bella's travel plans."

"She was going to Europe with Jake," Jenny told the others.

"Sam wanted to get the money from Bella before she eloped. He decided to do something to delay the wedding."

"So he didn't want to kill Bella?" Jenny was sad.

Jason shook his head.

"Bella was the only one who had shown him kindness. He loved her. He just wanted to make her sick for a while."

"How did he do it?" Heather asked. "Was it easy?"

"Bella never suspected him," Jason relayed. "He handed her a drink garnished with poisonous flowers."

"Calvin must have seen him," Jenny guessed. "Did he confront Sam with the truth?"

Jason leaned back in his chair and rubbed his eyes.

"Calvin had a photo of Sam handing over the drink to Bella. It's not clear if he knew what it was. Sam didn't want to take any risks."

"So he decided to stage Calvin's suicide?"

"Sam knew Calvin was a bit obsessed with Bella. He thought the police would pin the blame on Calvin when they saw the wall full of Bella's photos."

"What about Jenny?" Heather cried. "Was he planning to kill her too?"

"When Jenny asked Sam about his wonder drug, he panicked. He thought Jenny already knew what he had done."

Jason looked at his wife.

"How much of those brownies did you eat?"

"I barely nibbled one," Jenny shrugged. "I was just being polite."

"You were lucky," Jason said hoarsely. "Who knows what would have happened if you had eaten more than that."

"What was this poison he was using?" Star asked. "Where did he find it?"

"Monkshood," Jason told them. "Police found some growing behind Sam's trailer."

"That's a known poison," Star muttered. "Why was he growing it? Did he always intend to use it on someone?"

"We'll never know that," Jason said. "There were a bunch of other plants, neatly planted in a patch behind the trailer. They must have gone into that wonder drug of his."

"Poor misguided boy." Betty Sue was sad. "Two young people have lost their lives because of him."

"Let's hope Bella can rest in peace now," Molly said. "You did it again, Jenny!"

"He apologized," Jason said with a grimace. "They say he was crying his heart out. He never meant to hurt anyone. But he couldn't stop once he started."

Jenny didn't know if Sam would ever be able to forgive himself. But she felt sorry for him. She looked around at her friends and family and said a silent prayer. She promised herself she would be more grateful for everything she had in life.

Epilogue

The Pelican Cove spring festival was in full swing. Tourists and locals milled around as the flaming ball of the sun hung low on the horizon.

Wide-eyed kids dragged their parents around, eager to sample the treats offered at every stall. A cotton candy booth did brisk business, spinning bright blue balls of spun sugar for eager customers.

Jenny dished out her special strawberry sundaes as fast as she could. The Magnolias were back at Seaview, helping Jason prep for dinner. A grand barbecue was planned and most of Jason's and Jenny's friends were invited.

"This is the last one," Jenny announced and looked up into a pair of familiar blue eyes.

She mutely handed over the ice cream to Adam and took a step back involuntarily.

"How are you, Jenny?" Adam asked softly.

Jenny was tongue tied.

"Are you happy?"

"You don't have the right to ask me that," Jenny whispered hoarsely.

"I made a big mistake," Adam said, ignoring the ice cream dripping down his hand. "Will you accept my apology?"

Jenny's eyes burned with tears of anger.

"I think you should go now."

"Don't do this, Jenny," Adam said, gripping her arm with one hand. "You and me, we are meant to be."

Jenny tried to struggle out of his grip.

"You can't spend your life with Jason. You don't love him."

"What do you know about love?" Jenny cried.

"He's saddled you with someone else's child. You are just a glorified baby sitter, Jenny."

"Don't you dare talk about Emily," Jenny glared. "Get out of my sight right now, Adam!"

"It's not too late," Adam said, flinging the melted ice cream to the ground. "Get an annulment. We can have a summer wedding."

Adam's eyes bore into Jenny's, compelling her to stare

right back. Adam whirled around without another word and stalked away. Within seconds, he was swallowed by the crowd.

Jenny shook like a leaf, her head reeling. She gripped the table with her hands, trying to summon the strength to brave this new storm in her life.

Thank you for reading this book. If you enjoyed this book, please consider leaving a brief review. Even a few words or a line or two will do.

As an indie author, I rely on reviews to spread the word about my book. Your assistance will be very helpful and greatly appreciated.

I would also really appreciate it if you tell your friends and family about the book. Word of mouth is an author's best friend, and it will be of immense help to me.

Many Thanks!

Author Leena Clover

http://leenaclover.com

leenaclover@gmail.com

http://twitter.com/leenaclover

https://www.facebook.com/leenaclovercozymysterybooks

Acknowledgements

I was amazed by the amount of interest this book generated. Many of you wrote to me and posted messages on social media asking about the release. I hope the book managed to live up to your expectations at least a bit.

I cannot thank everyone enough for all the interest and appreciation.

A big thank you to all my beta readers and early reviewers for their valued feedback. Many thanks to my loving family for their tremendous support and encouragement.

I am grateful you are here. You motivate me to write more.

Join my Newsletter

Get access to exclusive bonus content, sneak peeks, giveaways and much more. Also get a chance to join my exclusive ARC group, the people who get first dibs on all my new books.

Sign up at the following link and join the fun.

Click here →
http://www.subscribepage.com/leenaclovernl

I love to hear from my readers, so please feel free to connect with me at any of the following places.

Website – http://leenaclover.com

Twitter – https://twitter.com/leenaclover

Facebook – http://facebook.com/leenaclovercozymysterybooks

Email – leenaclover@gmail.com

Other books by Leena Clover

Pelican Cove Cozy Mystery Series –

Strawberries and Strangers

Cupcakes and Celebrities

Berries and Birthdays

Sprinkles and Skeletons

Waffles and Weekends

Muffins and Mobsters

Parfaits and Paramours

Truffles and Troubadours

Sundaes and Sinners

Dolphin Bay Cozy Mystery Series –

Raspberry Chocolate Murder

Orange Thyme Death

Apple Caramel Mayhem

Meera Patel Cozy Mystery Series -

Gone with the Wings

A Pocket Full of Pie

For a Few Dumplings More

Back to the Fajitas

Christmas with the Franks

Made in the USA
Columbia, SC
23 October 2023

24851869R00157